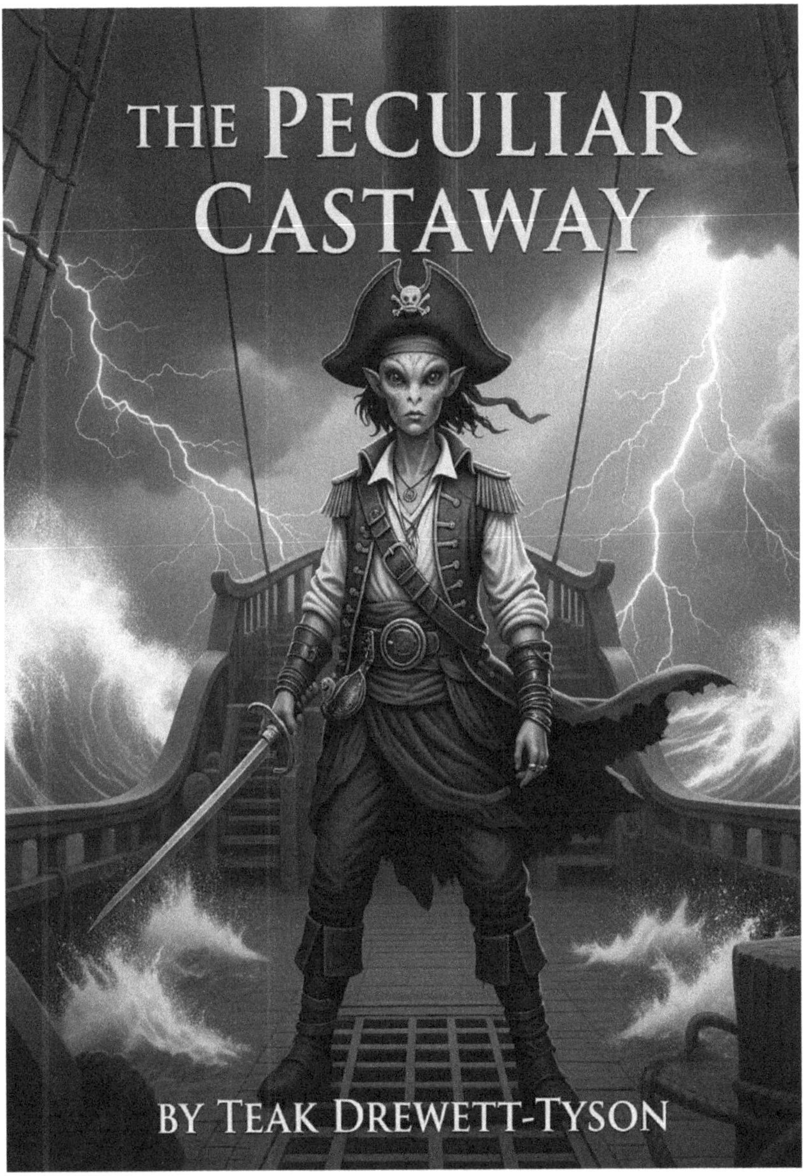

THE PECULIAR CASTAWAY

BY TEAK DREWETT-TYSON

The Peculiar Castaway

By

Teak Drewett-Tyson

Dedication

For my wife and son, the true loves of my life. Your boundless love and steadfast support, especially when I was at my lowest, fueled every word to everyone who stood by me, my deepest gratitude.

Acknowledgments

To my incredible family and friends: This book exists because you let me be me. Thank you for the mental sanity checks (or at least pretending I had some) and for the physical support that kept me fueled and functional. You're the true heroes who fostered the weirdness within.

And to all the teachers who didn't just tolerate my boundless imagination, but actively encouraged it: thank you. You never shut down my creativity; you nourished it. This book is for all of you who saw the oddball and helped it fly.

Contents

Prologue: The Omni-Sight – A New Assignment

For countless cycles, the Vydar had existed as silent chroniclers of the cosmos. Their inherent forms were tall, elegant beings with light grey skin, physical bodies distinct from the more volatile life they observed. Emotion, for The Vydar, was merely a complex data variable, never an experience. Their purpose was absolute: to observe, to meticulously chart the rise and fall of civilizations, mapping the subtle shifts in planetary energies, and listening to the very breath of nascent stars.

Project Terra was one such grand endeavor. A comprehensive, multi-spectral observation focused on a highly dynamic world classified as 'Type 3 Planetary Evolution - Primitive Terrestrial Dominance.' Its dominant species, 'Humans,' who inhabited the world known as Earth, were a fascinating anomaly – beings of fierce passions and bewildering complexity.

Orbiting far above this vibrant sphere was The Omni-Sight, Vydar's state-of-the-art sentinel. It was a vessel dedicated entirely to the tireless processing of cosmic information, a silent, all-seeing eye.

Xylar was new to The Omni-Sight. A young scientist, recently arrived from his home world, had been assigned to Project Terra to lend his fresh perspective to the vast flow of data. His prior experience was limited, his direct assignments confined to theoretical simulations and the analysis of impersonal probe readings. The intricate rhythms of Human life, the baffling nuances of their civilization, were entirely new to him, a vast, unexplored frontier of information. He found himself quickly immersed in the torrent of data – social structures, technological advancements, artistic expressions, the very pulse of Earth's complex ecosystems.

He had not been aboard The Omni-Sight for long when a unique opportunity arose: a solo mission. A specialized, low-impact deployment for closer observation of a specific, particularly intriguing region of the Human world. It was an unexpected chance for direct data acquisition, a test of his fledgling observational skills.

As the cycles turned, Xylar prepared for his assignment. He was a silent, unseen presence, meticulously preparing to collect data, fulfilling his Prime Directive. The vast, blue-green world of Terra continued its ceaseless churn of life, blissfully unaware of the advanced intelligence that watched its every breath. The observation continued.

Chapter 1: Crash Landing

The Stardust Wanderer was a whisper of advanced Vydar technology, a sleek, personal observation vessel specifically configured for high-density data acquisition within planetary atmospheres. Xylar, now fully immersed in his solo assignment, guided it silently above the swirling blue-green orb of Earth. His objective was a focused, low-impact observation of a peculiar, volatile species designated "Human," concentrating on their localized social structures and perplexing emotional displays within a specific continental region. He meticulously adjusted his sensory inputs, cataloging their chaotic interactions with the detached precision his people cultivated.

Nothing in his exhaustive Vydar training or the vast data archives of The Omni-Sight, however, could have prepared him for a Caribbean hurricane.

One moment, the Stardust Wanderer was cutting through the upper atmosphere with effortless grace. The next, it was being pummeled by atmospheric forces so immense, so utterly untamed, that his vessel – designed for precision in the vacuum of space, not raw planetary fury – groaned in protest. Alarms shrieked, a cacophony of urgent, unfamiliar warnings that tore through the calm logic of his mind. Xylar felt a dizzying, sickening lurch as automated systems fought a losing battle against the planet's raw fury, the very air itself seeming to become a solid, crushing fist.

He awoke to the jarring, abrasive sensation of sand grinding against newly formed skin. His last conscious memory was the Stardust Wanderer's structural integrity collapsing, followed by a searing flash. Now, the vessel was a mangled, unrecognizable husk, its once-pristine hull torn open like crumpled foil, half-submerged in the turquoise shallows. The air was thick with a strange, humid warmth, and the alien scent of unknown flora filled his nasal passages. A harsh, yellow sun beat down relentlessly. With a final, sputtering surge of energy, the ship's dying AI had completed its last, desperate task: synthesizing a biological interface – a human disguise – for Xylar and delivering a critically condensed data burst into his neural net. "Designated Species: Human. Dominant characteristic: Chaos. Primary Objective: Blend." Then, silence. Utter, terrifying silence.

Xylar, or rather, the surprisingly bipedal, slightly sun-burnt, and somewhat gangly form he now inhabited, pushed himself up. He felt... heavy. And soft. And parts of him seemed to jiggle unsettlingly when he moved. He stumbled towards the wreckage, the hot sun beating down on his unfamiliar scalp, his limbs feeling strangely disconnected from his will. His primary impulse was to restore his research vessel, to return to the ordered logic of his mission.

He spent the first day and a half in a desperate, futile attempt to reactivate the Stardust Wanderer. Each effort was met with groans of tortured metal, fizzles of failing circuits, or the eerie silence of dead technology. Yet, through sheer persistence, he managed to coax a few more fractured data packets from the dying ship's memory banks. They flickered into his mind, incomplete and contextless, adding to his profound confusion. He learned of "Boxing," a "competitive ritual" of self-inflicted harm, and "Eating," a method of "oral ingestion." His most perplexing acquisition was a series of audio files: "Primary Communication Method: Vocalization. Sample: Common Human Phrase – 'Ahoy, matey!'" He spent an hour attempting to "converse" with a crab using this phrase, perplexed by its lack of response.

By the third day, hunger gnawed at him, a sharp, unfamiliar pain, and his "human" body ached in unfamiliar ways. The sun beat down relentlessly, making him feel sluggish and weak. He lay on the hot sand, contemplating the utter futility of his mission, when a new sound reached his ears – rhythmic, clanking, the faint slap of canvas. He cautiously peered through the dense foliage.

Chapter 2: Aboard the Sea Serpent: The Education of Xylar

A small vessel, propelled by a great white sheet of canvas, cut through the turquoise waters, growing larger with each passing moment. On its deck, a motley collection of weathered faces and boisterous laughs filled the air, a cacophony of Human vocalizations. Xylar, driven by a primal, insistent need for sustenance he now understood as "hunger," and a scientist's bewildered curiosity, pushed through the dense foliage at the water's edge, clutching a half-eaten, suspiciously slimy fish. His newly synthesized skin, still aching and unfamiliar, felt raw against the humid air.

The rough-and-tumble humans aboard the schooner Sea Serpent initially mistook his bewildered stares, his gaunt appearance, and his odd vocalizations for a severe case of sunstroke. Their captain, a formidable woman named Elara, with a laugh that could rival a foghorn and a heart just as vast, took pity on him. "Well, look what the tide dragged in!" she boomed, her voice resonating with an unfamiliar warmth. She extended a calloused hand, thick and strong, and Xylar, recalling the ship's dying AI's "handshake" protocol, grasped it with an enthusiasm that nearly dislocated her shoulder. "Ahoy, matey!" he croaked, the phrase feeling clunky on his new tongue but sounding exactly as the data burst had indicated.

Elara merely chuckled. The crew, finding his earnest, if clumsy, attempts endearing, quickly nicknamed him "Xy."

Life aboard the Sea Serpent became Xylar's intensive, often hilarious, crash course in humanity. The vessel itself was a living entity of creaking timber and salt-laced rope, its very scent a complex new data point – a mix of tar, old fish, and human perspiration. The sounds were a constant symphony: the slap of waves against the hull, the groan of strained ropes in the wind, the rhythmic creak of the mast, and the ceaseless chatter of the crew. This was not the pristine, silent efficiency of a Vydar vessel; it was a rough, vibrant, undeniably organic machine.

He soon learned a few more faces among the ship's thirty-odd souls. There was Jax, a burly, good-natured quartermaster with a perpetually amused grin and an unfortunate habit of spitting tobacco juice into the wind. Lys, younger than most, was nimble and quick on the rigging, her laughter a bright contrast to the older sailors' gruffness. Old Man Tiber, the cook, a grizzled figure who seemed more sea-weathered than the ship itself, always smelled faintly of burnt stew and muttered obscure warnings about the deeper currents of the ocean.

There was also Kael, a muscular deckhand with a booming laugh and an endless supply of shanties, whose sheer brute force seemed to replace any need for elegant Vydar mechanics in handling heavy loads. Each crew member presented a unique set of behaviors for Xylar to log, from their peculiar eating habits in the cramped mess hall – involving loud chewing and even louder storytelling – to their bewildering rituals of leisure like "knucklebones," where Xylar's precise calculations were met with accusations of "witchcraft."

When asked by Elara if he'd seen her missing spyglass, he reported its precise location in the bilge, a precise fact he had observed during his brief time on the beach. It took her a patient hour to explain the nuanced art of a "convenient truth," a concept that directly contradicted the Vydar Prime Directive of objective data. Every interaction was a new data point, every laugh a complex emotional readout, every shared meal a baffling ritual of communal ingestion. The chaos, as the AI had predicted, was truly dominant, yet within it, Xylar began to discern nascent patterns of loyalty and a strange, compelling warmth.

Chapter 3: Uncanny Instincts and a Growing Respect

Days bled into a bewildering sequence of sun-drenched mornings and star-strewn nights aboard the Sea Serpent. Xylar continued his meticulous observation, recording the complex behavioral patterns of humans at sea. He noted Elara's authoritative but fair leadership, Jax's pragmatic wisdom, Lys's boundless energy, Old Man Tiber's quiet superstitions, and Kael's unwavering joviality. The ship itself, a symphony of creaks and groans, had begun to feel less like a jarring cacophony and more like a predictable, if inefficient, system. He was learning their currents, literally and figuratively.

Despite his frequent social blunders – the awkward attempts at humor, the overly literal interpretations of common idioms – Xylar's alien mind began to prove surprisingly useful. One sweltering afternoon, with the ship becalmed under a sky of blinding blue, the Human crew sweltered in the heavy stillness. For Xylar, however, his Vydar sensory inputs registered a distinct, rapid drop in atmospheric pressure, a change far too subtle for any human instrument or perception. He pointed frantically towards the deceptively clear horizon, his voice still a touch too flat, too precise for human ears. "Wind... incoming... velocity... high!"

Elara, initially skeptical of his urgent but unscientific pronouncements, saw the stark conviction in his otherwise impassive black eyes. There was no cloud, no ripple on the water, yet Xy's intensity was undeniable. Taking a calculated risk on the peculiar castaway's odd certainty, she barked orders: "Reef the sails! All hands, make fast!" Minutes later, the ocean surface ahead erupted as a sudden, violent squall descended, hitting with the force of a solid wall. The Sea Serpent bucked and strained, but held firm. Later that day, they passed a less fortunate schooner, its mast snapped like a dry twig. "Good call, lad. Yer eyes are sharper than a shark's tooth," Elara muttered, clapping him on the shoulder with a force that rattled his still-unfamiliar human frame. From then on, she began to trust his uncanny "instincts."

On another occasion, navigating a treacherous coral reef system, the Sea Serpent threaded its way through seemingly clear channels. Xylar, recalling a brief geological data burst from his ship's last moments — information he hadn't even consciously processed until now — recognized a specific, subtle rock formation far below the glittering surface, a pattern of density and mineral composition that spelled submerged danger. "Danger… shallow… left," he stated, pointing with an unwavering finger. Though the visible waters appeared safe, Elara, remembering the squall, trusted him. She rerouted, safely bypassing a hidden shoal that would have ripped the hull open. "How'd ye know that, Xy?" Barnaby, a burly deckhand, asked, wide-eyed. Xylar simply offered a slight, new shrug, finding it an efficient Human gesture for "no logical explanation comprehensible to you."

His utility wasn't limited to predicting natural hazards. During a scurvy outbreak, when several crew members weakened and their teeth loosened, Xylar subtly suggested stocking up on "citrus spheres" from a trading post they approached – a vague recollection from a fragment of downloaded nutritional data. Elara, though bewildered by his odd terminology, acquired the fruit. The rapid recovery that followed seemed nothing short of miraculous to the ailing sailors. The crew, observing these inexplicable interventions, began to see Xylar less as a bewildered castaway and more as a strange, silent oracle whose peculiar insights, though baffling, kept them safe and healthy. A quiet, growing respect, born of survival, began to replace their initial amusement.

Chapter 4: Adventures and Bonds

Life on the Sea Serpent, buoyed by the growing, albeit bewildered, respect for Xylar's uncanny instincts, settled into a rhythm of sun-drenched days and star-filled nights. The constant thrum of the ship and the ceaseless activity of the crew became increasingly legible patterns in Xylar's mind, a complex system he was learning to navigate with surprising fluidity. Despite his underlying mission of objective observation for the Vydar Collective, Xylar found himself genuinely drawn into the simple pleasures of Human existence, logging them with a curious, almost nascent, enjoyment.

Bustling port towns became new, vibrant data environments, each a sensory explosion. In Port Royal, the cacophony of voices, the bewildering array of goods, and the dizzying press of bodies overwhelmed his senses. He was profoundly baffled by "bartering," attempting to trade a perfectly symmetrical seashell for a strand of lustrous pearls, a logical exchange of aesthetically pleasing objects. It took Elara, with a patient sigh, to explain the baffling concept of "intrinsic value," a cultural construct tied to rarity and demand rather than inherent physical perfection. Back on board, he learned to tie rudimentary knots, his alien dexterity often making them too perfect, leading Jax to grumble about "fancy work" that defied common sense. He consistently brought bountiful fish catches, simply by pointing where the net should be cast, sensing the subtle electrical impulses of marine life long before any Human could. The crew, now trusting his strange pronouncements, would follow his silent direction without question, often marveling at the sudden abundance.

Their voyages were punctuated by vivid stops. In a small, nameless fishing village nestled against emerald cliffs, Xylar observed a "celebration ritual" involving elaborate costumes and synchronized dances, meticulously logging the complex social dynamics while subtly mimicking a rhythmic foot tap. On another occasion, while trading for fresh water in a bustling harbor, Kael challenged a local strongman to an arm-wrestling contest. Xylar, analyzing the minute muscular contractions and leverage points, silently communicated a subtle adjustment in Kael's stance. The cheers that erupted when Kael unexpectedly pinned his opponent and Kael's booming laugh as he clapped Xylar on the back were logged as "positive social reinforcement."

One memorable trip led to the discovery of an intensely sweet, vibrantly colored fruit in a forgotten cove. Intrigued, Xylar ingested a quantity far exceeding Human tolerance. The liquid sweetness overloaded his internal systems, causing a strange, pleasant fuzziness to spread through him, culminating in an unexpected physiological reaction: whenever he sneezed, he emitted a series of musical whistles. "Bless you, Xy, sounds like a dying tea kettle!" Kael quipped, roaring with laughter as Xylar's next sneeze produced a trilling crescendo.

Later, in a dimly lit tavern in Tortuga, Xylar had his infamous first encounter with rum. He had observed the crew's consumption of the liquid, noting the erratic but often convivial behavioral shifts. Curiosity, a driving force even for a Vydar, compelled him to try. The liquid burned, then sent a strange, pleasant fuzziness through him, loosening the rigid parameters of his Vydar logic. He found himself laughing, a genuine, unforced sound that resonated through his unfamiliar human chest. He attempted to jig, flailing his limbs in an uncoordinated, endearing dance that sent tankards clattering and caused the entire tavern to erupt in cheers and laughter around him. He woke the next morning with a pounding "headache," a sensation he logged as "Post-Alcoholic Disorientation," but also a new, inexplicable warmth in his core. These strange sensations, these shared moments of chaos and mirth, were forming bonds he hadn't anticipated, reshaping his mission in ways he couldn't yet comprehend.

One evening, under a sky ablaze with stars that seemed almost close enough to touch, Elara, her voice surprisingly soft, began to hum a slow, mournful sea shanty. She taught Xylar the words, patiently repeating the verses until he grasped their phonetic structure. Xylar, in turn, tried to hum along, his alien vocal cords, though now adapted for human speech, producing a series of ethereal, almost harmonic tones that were unlike any sound the crew had ever heard. The Vydar's natural precision lent his humming an unearthly purity, and the crew found it captivating, often falling silent to listen, their rough voices replaced by his strange, beautiful melody. Elara and her crew, these chaotic, boisterous, deeply loyal humans, had become more than subjects of observation; they were his family, their camaraderie a balm to his alien solitude. He learned "friendship," a warmth far more profound than any data packet could convey, a connection that resonated deeper than any Vydar algorithm. For the first time since his crash, adrift on a strange world in a borrowed body, Xylar felt a profound sense of belonging. He had a place.

Chapter 5: The Black Kraken: A Shadow on the Horizon

The warmth of camaraderie, the profound, newfound sense of belonging Xylar had discovered among the Sea Serpent crew, was brutally fleeting. One brutal morning, as the sun clawed its way above the horizon, painting the sky in fiery oranges and soft purples, a chilling sight appeared on the distant waters: a black flag unfurling against the dawn sky. It bore a stylized, grotesque squid, its tentacles writhing around a stark white skull. The chill that ran down Xylar's newly accustomed spine wasn't from the crisp sea air; it was a deeper, more profound tremor, a premonition his Vydar senses interpreted as a fundamental disruption in the local energetic field, a discordant hum of imminent, systemic violence.

Elara, standing grim-faced at the helm, her jaw tight, her usual boisterousness replaced by a chilling stillness, identified it: "The Black Kraken." Her voice was a low growl, barely audible above the rising wind. Around the deck, the crew, once lively, fell into a stunned, terrified silence, their faces paling, hands instinctively reaching for weapons or crossing themselves. The very air seemed to thicken with dread.

Tales of the Black Kraken were whispered in every port, a grim legend etched into the fear-filled hearts of sailors across these seas. Its captain, Captain "Redtooth" Malakor, was not merely fierce; he was a force of nature, a hurricane of calculated cruelty that left nothing but destruction in his wake. His name was uttered with the same trepidation reserved for typhoons or sea monsters. It was said his smile could curdle milk, revealing teeth filed to points and forever stained crimson, a habit he cultivated from a monstrous, rumored pact made in the depths, or from the fresh blood of his first betrayed captain, depending on which terrified whisper you believed. His eyes, like flint chips, held no warmth, only a predatory intelligence and a chilling, boundless malice that had consumed him since his ruthless ascent from common deckhand to undisputed terror of the seas. His signature act, the one that ensured his terrifying reputation and drove terrified whispers across a thousand leagues, was to leave exactly one survivor from every ship he plundered. Just one, a broken messenger, adrift or marooned, to carry the tale of his terror, to spread the plague of fear that was his most potent weapon. He didn't seek gold alone; he sought to dismantle hope, to leave a void.

The Black Kraken itself was a monstrous marvel, a three-masted brigantine built for unholy speed and utter intimidation. Its hull was painted a profound, light-absorbing black that seemed to drink in the very dawn, making it appear like a gaping maw, a predatory shadow moving effortlessly across the waves. Its sails, dark as a moonless night, billowed with unnatural efficiency, catching every whisper of wind, carrying it with a speed no other vessel could match. Its rigging, though perfectly maintained, had a skeletal quality, like a giant, predatory beast. Ominous carvings of fanged sea creatures and tormented figures adorned its bow and stern, silent witnesses to its grim purpose.

Its crew were fitting inhabitants for such a vessel: vile creatures, scarred and brutish, their faces a tapestry of old wounds and malicious grins. They were a collection of cutthroats, renegades, and the truly depraved, drawn to Malakor not just by coin, but by the promise of unfettered brutality. Their shouts were not boisterous laughs but guttural barks, their movements efficient and predatory. They reveled in the screams of their victims, finding a perverse joy in the suffering they inflicted. They were as much a part of the Kraken's terror as its captain, a living extension of his cruelty, driven by a shared, insatiable hunger for chaos and destruction. For Xylar, this was a new, horrifying data set, a level of destructive, organized chaos that surpassed anything he had yet observed. He logged the cold knot in his stomach, a sensation he now recognized as pure, unadulterated fear.

Chapter 6: The Attack

The warmth of the rising sun was instantly obliterated. The roar of The Black Kraken's cannons was not just a sound; it was the physical manifestation of an apocalypse, a deafening concussion that vibrated through the very bones of the Sea Serpent. A synchronized, devastating broadside tore into their starboard side, not once, but in a thunderous volley. Wood splintered with the crack of thunder, erupting in lethal shrapnel that whistled through the air. Canvas ripped with a sound like monstrous tearing flesh, sails shredding into tattered ribbons. The acrid scent of gunpowder instantly filled Xylar's nasal passages, sharp and burning, mingling with the bitter tang of shattered timber and the coppery smell of freshly drawn blood.

"Brace yourselves, lads! Hold fast!" Elara's bellow cut through the cacophony, a desperate counterpoint to the ship's death cries, even as a spray of splinters exploded near her head. The deck beneath Xylar's feet shuddered violently, listing sharply. Crewmates scrambled, their faces etched with a raw fear Xylar logged even as his own new human heart hammered in his chest. Lys scrambled up a surviving mast, frantically trying to secure a tattered sail. Jax, axe already in hand, roared defiance, bracing for impact. Old Man Tiber, surprisingly nimble, was already throwing buckets of water onto a smoldering patch of deck.

Xylar, his youthful face etched with a bewildering mix of confusion and fierce loyalty, clutched the cutlass that Kael, his face grim and streaked with soot, had thrust into his hand. The blade felt impossibly heavy and awkward, an extension of his arm he had no data for. He didn't understand "fighting" in its chaotic, brutal human form, but he understood the overriding directive to protect his family. He tried to mimic Kael's stance, his movements clumsy, his grip unsure. "What… what do I do?" he whispered, his voice thin against the gale of violence. "Swing! Hit something that ain't us!" Kael yelled back, his own eyes darting, assessing the damage.

Before another broadside could obliterate them, the pirate brigantine, impossibly fast, swung alongside. Grappling hooks, tipped with cruel barbs, arced through the air, embedding themselves in the Sea Serpent's railings with sickening thuds. A horde of figures, dark and indistinct against the glaring sun, swarmed aboard. They were a tide of cutlasses, pistols, and primal cruelty, their war cries guttural and chilling.

The deck became a swirling maelstrom of steel and screams. A hulking brute, his face a roadmap of scars, lunged at Xylar, a cutlass glinting menacingly. Xylar, still grasping the unfamiliar blade, deflected the blow with a desperate, instinctual flinch, but stumbled backward over a loose coil of rope, barely avoiding a swift chop that would have cleaved his head. Silas, a wizened deckhand, appeared out of nowhere, yanking Xylar back by the collar. "Watch yourself, lad! You'll lose your head!" he barked, driving his own blade into Xylar's attacker with a wet crunch. Xylar, still dazed, ducked under a swinging arm, tripped over another rope, and narrowly missed a thrust thanks to Kael's quick shove that sent the pirate stumbling. He saw crewmates fall, their cries abruptly silenced, their vibrant life energies extinguishing in a flash that only he could perceive. His hands, still clutching the cutlass, trembled with a burgeoning, terrible fear, a data point he was logging with horrifying clarity: pure terror.

The Sea Serpent crew fought with the desperate courage of the damned. Elara, a whirlwind of steel, parried blows with a skill honed by years of survival. Jax, with his axe, was a furious anchor in the chaos, his body a bulwark against the tide. Lys, agile as a monkey, swung from rigging, dropping onto pirates' heads, then disappearing back into the fray. Old Man Tiber, wielding a sharpened belaying pin, fought with a surprising ferocity, spitting curses. But they were outnumbered, outgunned, and facing an enemy utterly devoid of mercy. The screams of the dying, the clash of steel, and the sickening thuds of bodies hitting the deck formed a grotesque symphony that assaulted Xylar's enhanced senses.

Then, a ripple of fresh, primal fear went through even the attacking pirates. A figure, impossibly tall and imposing, leaped onto the Sea Serpent's blood-slicked deck from the Black Kraken's railing. His coat black as pitch seemed to drink the light, his hair tangled like sea wrack, a cruel, shark-like grin splitting his face, revealing teeth filed into points. Captain "Redtooth" Malakor had joined the fray. His presence seemed to suck the very air from the deck, replacing it with an oppressive, malevolent chill that Xylar's Vydar sensors registered as a palpable aura of destructive intent. The last vestiges of hope among the Sea Serpent crew flickered and died.

"Xy!" Elara's voice cut through the din, sharp with desperate command, a lifeline in the madness. She was locked in a grim struggle with two hulking pirates, but her eyes fixed on him, wide with fierce, protective love that resonated deeply within Xylar's core. "Get below deck! Hide, lad! Now! That's an order, Xy, ye hear me?! Now!" The absolute authority in her voice, coupled with the profound emotional resonance he now associated with her, compelled him. He stumbled towards the nearest hatch, his useless cutlass dragging on the deck. The sounds of battle — screams, clash of steel, sickening thuds — echoed behind him, magnified by the confined space as he descended, searing themselves into his memory as a terrifying new dataset of Human conflict and loss. He heard Elara's roar of defiance, a final defiant cry, before it was abruptly silenced, replaced by a chilling, triumphant cackle from above.

Chapter 7: Redtooth's Cruelty

Rough, calloused hands, reeking of salt, stale sweat, and the metallic tang of fresh blood, dragged Xylar back up onto the gore-slicked deck. His head swam, his human body protesting the violence, but his Vydar mind, though reeling, desperately sought to process the raw data of chaos and despair. He was thrown, unceremoniously, to his knees before Captain Malakor, who seemed to swell to monstrous proportions, towering over him like a predatory shadow against the ruined mast.

Malakor's voice, a low, guttural rasp, grated like stones grinding together. "Well, well. A mere whelp. You're just a child, aren't you? Did you truly think you could stand against the Black Kraken? Did you think you could challenge me?" He chuckled, a deep, mirthless sound that scraped against Xylar's very being. "I am the storm, boy. I am the very terror of the seas, and all who sail them are but flotsam at my whim."

As Malakor's cruel words echoed, Xylar's mind raced, a torrent of Vydar calculations clashing with the burgeoning, illogical human emotions now writhing within him. He processed the probability of survival, the destructive force of Malakor's crew, and the impossibility of resistance. His mission: observe, do not interfere. His nature: logical, analytical, detached. But the memories of laughter, of Elara's warmth, of Kael's booming jokes, of the crew's camaraderie, flared like dying stars. Could he intervene? Could he access the full spectrum of his Vydar abilities – perception manipulation, localized energy bursts – and somehow save them? The data was clear: exposure of his true nature would mean the utter compromise of Project Terra, drawing unwanted attention to Earth, potentially leading to its destruction or subjugation by more hostile Vydar factions. It was a choice between the immediate, desperate love for his fleeting family and the prime directive to protect an entire species from galactic notice. The calculus of sacrifice was brutal. His newly awakened sense of loyalty warred with aeons of Vydar logic. And the cold, undeniable conclusion surfaced: he could not save them all, not without condemning far more. His hand, still clutched around the useless cutlass, trembled. The choice was made, a crushing weight of inaction.

Malakor gestured around the ravaged deck, sweeping his hand over the broken, motionless bodies of the Sea Serpent crew, a grotesque tapestry of defiance and despair. "This is what true fear looks like! This is what happens to those who dare defy Redtooth Malakor! This is my message, painted in blood across the waves!" He paused, his gaze locking on Xylar, an unnerving intensity that promised no escape. "And now, for my... tradition. My little gift to the fools who still cling to hope.

Every ship I take, I leave one alive. Just one. One to tell the tale. To spread the fear."

He barked orders, and his vile crew, with grotesque enthusiasm, began the gruesome work. One by one, the remaining Sea Serpent crew, those clinging to life in the splintered wreckage, were dragged forward. Xylar, forced to watch, felt a cold knot of horror tighten in his gut, a sickening despair he meticulously logged even as his stomach churned. He saw Jax, the burly quartermaster, his face a mask of furious defiance, swiftly silenced. He saw Lys, her vibrant laughter replaced by a choked cry, disappear into the brutality. He saw Old Silas spit defiance, a last, brave gesture, before his gruesome fate was met with the flash of a blade. The air filled with dying gasps and the triumphant cackles of the pirates. And then, there was only Elara.

She was dragged before Malakor, her face bruised and bloodied, but her spirit unbroken, her eyes still holding a fierce, protective spark of fire. Her gaze, filled with an unfathomable depth of emotion, met Xylar's across the deck. "Xy," she said, her voice hoarse but clear, cutting through the echoes of screams. "You… you were the best thing that ever happened to this old ship. My son. Don't… don't let this break you. Live, Xy. Live for us."

Malakor sneered, a cruel twist of his crimson-stained lips. "Sentimental to the end, eh, Captain? A touching moment for the boy to witness."

With a swift, brutal motion, he raised his cutlass, its blade catching the dim light. Xylar, abandoning all logic, all directives, all fear for himself, lunged forward, a primal scream tearing from his throat, a sound born of pure, desperate anguish he never knew he could produce. But rough, iron-hard hands, belonging to Malakor's crew, instantly restrained him, crushing his futile resistance, forcing his eyes open. He watched, helpless, as Malakor brought the blade down. The world went black, not just from the stunning impact of a boot to his head that sent him sprawling, but from the searing, unbearable pain in his soul. The last thing he heard before oblivion claimed him was Malakor's triumphant, chilling laughter echoing across the silent, bloody deck.

Chapter 8: A Bitter Dawn, A New Purpose

When Xylar awoke, his head throbbed, a dull, relentless ache behind his eyes. His body was a symphony of unfamiliar pains – raw scrapes, bruised ribs, the gnawing emptiness in his stomach. He was lying at the bottom of a small, cramped dinghy, adrift. The sun beat down mercilessly, a golden disc in an indifferent sky, and his throat was parched, his mouth dry as dust. He pushed himself to a sitting position, his vision swimming, and stared at the horizon, dreading what he knew, with a cold certainty, he would see.

The Sea Serpent was gone. No longer a beacon of laughter and life. Only a distant, burning pyre, a thin column of black smoke climbing into the pristine morning sky, slowly, agonizingly sinking beneath the vast, indifferent waves, taking his family, his warmth, his entire found world with it. In the distance, the Black Kraken, its menacing black sails full and arrogant, was disappearing, a tiny, hateful speck on the horizon. The faint, horrifying sounds of the pirates' victory celebrations faintly reached his ears, carried on the breeze like a final, mocking cackle. Xylar was alone. Adrift. A solitary, grieving speck on an endless blue canvas, filled with a cold, burning, all-consuming rage. His Vydar mind struggled to process this new, overwhelming dataset: grief. It was a system overload, a profound corruption of all positive emotional algorithms, leaving behind only a void. The emptiness was a physical weight, heavier than any gravity well. He stared at the horizon, his logical circuits screaming for a solution, but finding none. Only the indifferent, endless blue.

Days blurred into a hazy, agonizing cycle of sun-baked skies and starlit, weeping nights. He drifted, utterly alone, suspended between the vastness of the ocean and the crushing void within him. His alien physiology allowed him to consume seawater without ill effect, filtering it on a molecular level, but the gnawing hunger was relentless, a constant reminder of his fragile, borrowed form. He managed to snatch a desperate fish from the ocean, consuming it raw, the act of survival purely mechanical. Each day, his youthful human form seemed to thin more, his eyes growing larger, haunted by visions of the massacre, by the faces of his family, by the triumphant, sneering face of Malakor.

Then, on the third dawn, a familiar silhouette emerged – a small, green smudge on the horizon. A flicker of something, a tiny spark of hope, ignited in his chest. A chance. Rescue. Any human contact. His heart, his battered, aching human heart, leaped. He paddled with renewed vigor, the thought of land, of human voices, driving his exhausted limbs, until the dinghy grated against familiar sand. He scrambled onto the beach, collapsing in exhaustion and relief. "I'm... I'm back!" he croaked, the words tasting like salt and sand.

But the cheer died in his throat, replaced by a fresh, sickening wave of despair. This wasn't just an island; it was the island. The very spot where his ship had crashed, where his desperate, clumsy attempts at human survival had begun. His old makeshift camp was still visible, littered with decaying remnants of his initial, bewildered struggle. The cosmic irony was a brutal slap: he had escaped the horrors of space only to find himself returned, irrevocably changed and utterly broken, to the very beginning of his short, tragic human journey. The circularity of it intensified the feeling of utter hopelessness, of being trapped by a cruel, inescapable fate.

He sat by the familiar indentation in the sand, his gaze fixed on the spot where the Stardust Wanderer had once lain, and began to build a small fire, the rhythmic strike of flint a hollow comfort. He stared into the nascent flames, and the memories came unbidden, vivid and achingly sweet: Elara's booming laugh, Kael's exasperation during his first knot lesson, Jax's gruff patience, Lys's boundless energy, their adventures in bustling ports, the sharp burn of his first rum, the crew's laughter at his clumsy dancing. He saw himself, a bewildered alien, slowly becoming Xy, a part of something larger than himself, a cherished member of a family. He remembered

Elara's gentle hand on his shoulder, her voice teaching him shanties under a blanket of stars, her eyes filled with a profound fondness he'd never known. He had been an anomaly on his homeworld, a scientist focused solely on data, detached and logical. Here, he had been loved.

As the happy memories danced in the firelight, they warped, twisting into grotesque shadows before his eyes. Joyous faces contorted into masks of terror. Sweet sounds curdled into desperate screams. Laughter became the triumphant, taunting cackles of Malakor's crew, ringing in his ears. The warmth of the rum was replaced by the cold, metallic tang of death, the scent of gunpowder, and the chilling presence of Malakor. Loving faces morphed into their final, anguished expressions, their silent pleas echoing in his mind.

Anger, cold and swift, a sudden, powerful surge of energy, extinguished the flickering warmth of the fire within him. It was a data packet of pure, focused wrath. He sprang up, kicking violently at the embers, sending sparks flying into the night. "No! No! You hear me?!" he screamed into the vast, uncaring ocean, his voice raw, ragged with a fury he'd never known. He thrashed at his makeshift camp, at the remnants of his old life, at the very sand beneath his feet, lashing out at his helplessness, at Malakor, at the universe itself. "They are gone! All of them! My family! You took them from me! Malakor! You monster!" He fell to his knees, burying his face in his hands, the grief a crushing, physical weight that threatened to pull him into the very earth.

But amidst the despair, the anger solidified into an unshakeable resolve, a cold, crystalline purpose. He lifted his head, his eyes burning with a fierce, newfound determination under the cold, indifferent stars. His voice, though still young, carried a new, steely edge, stripped bare of its former alien detachment.

"I am Xylar," he declared, his voice echoing over the waves, a solemn, terrible vow, "and I was sent here to observe. To understand. And now I understand." He clenched his fists, the strength of his resolve radiating through his gaunt frame. "You think you rule the waves, Malakor? You think fear is your greatest weapon? You left one survivor. One to spread your terror. But you made a mistake. A fatal error. You left me." He rose to his feet, a gaunt, furious figure silhouetted against the nascent light of dawn, every fiber of his being now aligned. "I will not spread your fear. I will spread your doom. I will learn this world, its chaos, its ruthlessness. I will master it. I will find you. And I will make you regret the day you ever set foot on the Sea Serpent. You wanted a messenger? You got one. A messenger of your destruction! This is my vow!"

Chapter 9: The Revenge of the Sea Serpent

The next morning, Xylar woke slowly, his youthful face grim, hardened by the resolve forged in the crucible of despair. His head still throbbed, and his body was a symphony of unfamiliar pains – raw scrapes, bruised ribs, the gnawing emptiness in his stomach. He pushed himself to his feet and walked along the shoreline, the indifferent waves licking at his bare feet. As he walked, his gaze, now sharper, more focused than ever, fell upon something glinting amidst the tangled seaweed: oddly shaped metal, fragmented bits of his former life, shards of the Stardust Wanderer. He picked up a twisted conduit, then a piece of a shattered navigational display, the familiar crystalline structure sparking recognition in his Vydar mind. He knelt, tracing the intricate patterns. He couldn't make it fly again as a starship. But what if he could make it fly among the waves? A grin, thin and sharp, stretched across his gaunt face, a predatory expression completely alien to his previous bewildered curiosity. He wouldn't leave this island a helpless victim again. He would take the remnants of his past and forge them, not just into a weapon for his retribution, but into a monument of his rage.

Over the next few weeks, Xylar became a tireless, solitary architect. His small, isolated camp transformed into a makeshift shipyard, a crucible of desperate ingenuity. His keen alien sight allowed him to discern minute structural weaknesses in natural materials and to perceive the inherent energy signatures within the salvaged alien tech. His advanced understanding of physics, metallurgy, and sub-molecular bonding guided his hands with uncanny precision. He improvised, using a sharpened rock as a cutting tool, hardened wood as a hammer, and manipulating elements with a finesse that defied the crude tools. He began cutting down the tallest, most resilient tropical trees, shaping the heavy, dense wood with uncanny precision, seeing the grain, the cellular structure, as clearly as a Vydar schematic.

Piece by piece, he painstakingly melded the alien metals with the sturdy timber, not merely joining them, but creating impossibly strong, seamless fusions through a subtle application of localized energy fields drawn from salvaged power cells. His dinghy, the vessel of his escape, became the foundation. Its form grew larger, its silhouette evolving into something unlike any human vessel – an elegant, almost predatory shape, blending organic curves of hardwood with sharp, angular lines of dark, burnished metal. He rigged a towering mast, its sails woven from salvaged canvas, subtly reinforced with interwoven alien filaments that gave them unparalleled strength, resilience against any storm, and aerodynamic efficiency far beyond conventional sailcloth, yet appearing to be perfectly ordinary, well-made sails.

From the core systems of the Stardust Wanderer, Xylar salvaged and re-purposed crucial components. Deep within the hull, integrated into the keel, he installed a sophisticated Vydar passive energy signature detection array. This was his early warning system, capable of detecting the unique thermal, electromagnetic, and vibrational patterns of other vessels from extreme distances, long before they broke the horizon. It hummed with a subtle, almost imperceptible energy that flowed through the ship. For offense, he painstakingly repurposed two of the Stardust Wanderer's smaller, auxiliary energy emitters. These weren't designed for planetary bombardment, but Xylar recalibrated them, drawing power from modified fusion cells salvaged from his old life-support system. He integrated them seamlessly into the bow, hidden behind retractable panels of dark hardwood, transforming them into potent, precise energy cannons. They wouldn't pulverize a mountain, but they could punch clean holes through a wooden hull or disable a mast with concentrated blasts, burning with a silent, focused intensity.

One sweltering afternoon, he discovered something massive wedged beneath driftwood: a remnant of a much larger vessel. As he worked, prying loose a particularly large plank, his breath hitched. The words, faded but unmistakable, were painted across its surface: SEA SERPENT. It was a piece of his ship, a piece of his family, a tangible link to the warmth he had lost. He clutched it as a sacred relic, a testament to the lives extinguished. He incorporated the Sea Serpent plank into the very heart of his new vessel, setting it proudly into the hull as a silent, defiant memorial to those he vowed to avenge.

Finally, after weeks of relentless, solitary labor that stripped him to bone and sinew, Xylar stood back. He was gaunt, his human clothes tattered, but his eyes glowed with fierce pride and grim satisfaction. Before him lay an engineering wonder: a swift, sleek hybrid, its hull a seamless blend of burnished alien alloys and dark, polished hardwood, a predator of the waves. A deep, almost imperceptible humming emanated from beneath its deck, the soft thrum of alien power contained. He spoke its name aloud, the words a vow echoing over the empty sea: "The Revenge of the Sea Serpent." It was finished.

Chapter 10: The Maiden Voyage: A Solo Struggle

Xylar stood at the polished wooden helm of his masterpiece, The Revenge of the Sea Serpent. The last rays of the sun were a fiery orange disc dipping below the horizon, casting long, triumphant shadows across the deck. The ship itself seemed to breathe beneath his feet, a subtle vibration of contained alien power, the integrated alloys gleaming like dark obsidian under the fading light. He ran a hand over the smooth, dark wood of the railing, feeling the latent energy, a profound fusion of two worlds. A surge of grim satisfaction, tinged with a raw, undeniable excitement, pulsed through him. This was it. His creation. His instrument of vengeance. Time to set sail.

His initial pride, however, quickly met the brutal realities of the open ocean. The sea, much like humanity, had its own unyielding lessons, and a lone Vydar, even one with enhanced strength and intellect, was no match for the sheer physical demands of a vessel this size. He moved to unfurl the enormous, reinforced sails — sails that looked like sturdy canvas, but promised unparalleled efficiency. The main sail, a vast expanse of heavy fabric, was a beast, resisting his every pull and tug with the stubbornness of a sleeping leviathan. He strained at the halyards, his muscles screaming in protest as the thick ropes chafed his palms. The sheer force required to haul the canvas aloft was immense, demanding the coordinated effort of a dozen strong men. He tried to apply a localized, Vydar-infused burst of strength, but the energy dissipated against the monumental scale of the sail, only serving to briefly numb his aching forearms. Clew lines, sheets, and braces became a tangled, complicated nightmare, defying the logical order his Vydar mind craved. The wind, instead of cooperating, seemed to conspire against him, snatching ropes from his grasp, whipping canvas into impossible snarls. He battled the rigging for hours, his body quickly covered in grime and sweat, a chorus of unfamiliar agony echoing through every fiber. Sweat, hot and salty, stung his eyes, blurring his vision, and in those moments of desperate, isolated struggle, he keenly missed the coordinated efforts of Jax, the patient guidance of Old Man Tiber, and the brawny assistance of Kael. He missed Elara's booming commands that could organize chaos into purposeful motion.

Steering proved equally challenging, a constant, high-stakes duel. The rudder, infused with subtle alien tech, responded with incredible, almost hyper-precision. It was designed for a crew of expert Vydar pilots, not a single, inexperienced human hand grappling with a wooden wheel. Maintaining a straight course in unpredictable currents and shifting winds was a delicate, agonizing art. He found himself wildly overcorrecting with the slightest touch, sending the ship veering wildly, then lagging disastrously behind the sea's shifts, the vessel listing drunkenly across the waves like a newborn colt. The sophisticated navigational display, a complex alien interface he'd resurrected from the Stardust Wanderer, poured torrents of data into his mind – current speeds, wind vectors, subsurface thermals, distant atmospheric pressure readings – but without a crew to assist with immediate physical adjustments, the raw information overwhelmed his ability to act. He was a master strategist without an army, a brilliant conductor lacking an orchestra.

Days of "sailing" blurred into a brutal, exhausting cycle. He learned to anticipate the rhythmic slap of waves against the hull, the groan of the timbers under strain, and the subtle shifts in the wind. But this learning came at a steep cost. He slept in short, restless bursts, often collapsing onto the deck where he stood, only to be jolted awake by a sudden lurch or a flapping sail. Each waking moment was a battle against the elements, the sheer scale of his undertaking, and his own mounting fatigue. There were near-disasters: a sudden squall that almost ripped a mast clear from its base, sending him scrambling, soaked and shivering, to secure lines; an unexpected sandbar he barely skirted, the alarm system's subtle hum escalating into an urgent thrumming warning that grated against his overtaxed senses. His human body was pushed beyond its limits, trembling with exertion. The humming from beneath the deck, the soft thrum of the ship's alien systems, was a constant reminder of the immense power he wielded, a power he was still struggling to master single-handedly. By any true sailor's definition, his solo journey was less "sailing" and more "determined drifting," a desperate dance between his incredible will and the unforgiving vastness of the ocean. Each aching muscle, each missed correction, each moment of bone-deep weariness, was a stark reminder of the family he had lost, and the solitary, immense task that lay before him.

Chapter 11: Whispers in Port

After what felt like an eternity, but was perhaps only a few days, a familiar coastline emerged from the morning mist. It was Tortuga. Xylar recognized the craggy cliffs, the distant, bustling harbor, even through the haze of exhaustion and the persistent ache in his bones. Every ripple of the Revenge of the Sea Serpent beneath him had been a silent conversation with pain, a testament to his own battered body and the makeshift repairs that held his unique vessel together. He coaxed the ship into a less conspicuous cove, a quiet inlet he knew from his earlier, greener days, dropping anchor with a soft splash that belied the monumental effort. The sudden silence of the calm water was a stark contrast to the storm that still raged within him.

Stepping onto solid ground, Xylar felt a profound tremor in his weary legs. He pulled his tattered, salt-stained cloak tighter, trying to blend into the morning shadows, to become just another anonymous figure on the waterfront. But the effort was futile. As he walked through the familiar, crowded streets, past stalls overflowing with exotic fruits and merchants hawking rough-spun cloth, the usual cacophony of vendors bellowing their wares, sailors shouting orders, and the distant clang of the blacksmith's hammer seemed to dim as he passed. Heads turned, slowly at first, then more rapidly. Whispers started, insidious as a creeping fog: "Isn't that...?" "The boy from the Sea Serpent?" "But they said everyone was lost..." Each hushed word, each speculative glance, felt like a barb, piercing the fragile shield of his resolve. He tried to ignore them, to focus on the grim purpose that propelled him, but the faces of Elara and his lost crew flashed in his mind. The whispers weren't just idle gossip; they were echoes of the tragedy that had claimed everything he knew, a chilling reminder of the life he'd left buried beneath the waves. A raw, hot knot of grief and fury tightened in his chest.

He pushed through the heavy wooden door of "The Salty Siren," the very tavern where he'd had his first taste of rum, a lifetime ago it seemed. The raucous noise inside—the drunken laughter, the clinking tankards, the off-key sea shanties that usually filled the smoky air—instantly died. Every eye, bleary or sharp, turned to him, following his every movement. The silence was thick with unspoken questions, with disbelief and a morbid curiosity. Xylar stood in the doorway, a spectral figure framed by the morning light, a ghost come back to haunt their easy assumptions of loss. The scent of stale ale, sweat, and cheap tobacco hung heavy, a familiar comfort and a fresh wound all at once.

Then, a burly figure detached himself from the bar, a tankard clutched in his large, scarred hand. It was Merrick, a one-eyed quartermaster Xylar had known since his first bewildered shore leave years ago. Merrick's weathered face, usually etched with a permanent scowl, was now slack with shock, his single eye wide with disbelief. "Xy! By the Kraken's beard, it is you!" Merrick boomed, his voice cracking with emotion, as he clapped Xylar heartily on the shoulder—a blow that nearly sent Xylar, weakened as he was, to his knees. "We heard... no survivors. We held a wake for Elara and all the brave souls lost. The rumors... terrible, lad. Here, take this. You look like you've seen the depths themselves." He shoved his own half-empty tankard into Xylar's hand. The rum burned a familiar, welcome path down his throat, momentarily dulling the phantom pains and the sharper sting of memory. Other familiar faces, some grim and solemn, some still wide-eyed with astonishment, began to approach hesitantly. They offered somber greetings, a few shaking his hand with a surprising tenderness, a silent acknowledgment of the hell he must have endured. The low hum of conversation slowly returned to the tavern, but it was a subdued murmur now, laced with awe and apprehension. They looked at him not just as a survivor, but as a living ghost, a stark, unwelcome reminder of the terrors of the sea and the ruthless hand of Malakor. His very presence was a challenge to their accepted reality, and a silent promise of what was to come.

Chapter 12: A Crew for Vengeance

Xylar, still clutching the tankard Merrick had given him, felt the warmth of the rum spread through his limbs, settling the tremors. He took a steadying breath, the initial shock having passed in the tavern. Now was the time for action. He found his voice, a low rumble that nonetheless cut through the lingering murmur of the room. He spoke about the attack, his gaze sweeping across the faces of the assembled pirates, many of whom he'd shared a drink with in better times.

"It was a clear day," he began, his voice gaining strength, raw with the memory. "The wind is fair, the sun bright. We were running light, just a few days out from port. Then they came. Black sails on the horizon, like a stain on the sky. Redtooth Malakor and his curs. They came fast, quiet as death." He described the initial volley of cannon fire that shredded the Sea Serpent's rigging, the boarding pikes that swarmed the decks, the sickening thud of cutlasses on flesh. He recounted the valiant, desperate fight Elara and her crew had put up, their defiant roars echoing even as they fell. He didn't shy from the details: the screams, the gurgling sounds as men choked on their own blood, the stench of gunpowder and fresh gore. "He revels in it," Xylar snarled, his voice a low growl. "He delights in terror. He didn't just raid us; he butchered us. Left nothing but splintered wood and a red stain on the waves. I was… lucky. Or perhaps cursed. Dragged clear of the wreck by a rogue current, clinging to a piece of driftwood. For days, I thought I was the only one left to remember what he did."

He saw shock, anger, and fear flicker across the faces before him – emotions he knew well. Some gripped their tankards tighter, knuckles white. Others averted their gaze, memories of their own losses or past encounters with Malakor clouding their eyes. The silence that followed his account was heavier than before, thick with the weight of shared experience and unspoken dread.

Then, Xylar delivered his intent, his gaze sweeping over the assembled pirates, a fire burning in his own eyes, brighter than any fear. "Redtooth Malakor thinks he's the king of the waves. He thinks fear is his only weapon. He left one survivor to spread his terror. But I will spread his destruction. I will hunt him down. And I will make him pay for what he did to Elara and her crew."

A few murmurs rippled through the crowd. Hunting Malakor was a fool's errand, a death wish whispered among the most hardened buccaneers. Malakor was a legend of brutality, whispered to be untouchable. Xylar knew this, so he pressed on, his voice shifting to a conspiratorial whisper, then rising with a newfound, calculated magnetism. He leaned into the lie, weaving it with threads of truth about his journey.

"You speak of Malakor's power. I speak of something greater. I have a vessel. A ship unlike any you've ever seen. Not just a ship," he asserted, his voice taking on a hypnotic cadence, "but a marvel. Built from remnants of a mighty, ancient wreck – one that held secrets lost to time. Imbued with energies that make its hull impervious, its speed a blur on the horizon. Faster than a gale, stronger than a storm. She practically sails herself, a living extension of my will." He painted a vivid picture of the Revenge of the Sea Serpent, exaggerating her qualities into the realm of myth, but carefully omitting any mention of Vydar technology or his alien heritage. He saw doubt in some eyes, but also a definite flicker of greedy interest, of wonder, of desperate hope in others. A ship like that? That changed the odds.

"But a ship, even one such as mine," he continued, his voice dropping to a serious tone, "is nothing without a crew. I need men. Men with courage, men with grit. Not just for plunder, though there will be plunder, I assure you. But for justice. For revenge."

The silence returned, but this time it was different. It was consideration, calculation. Heads slowly turned, not just to Xylar, but to each other. Hunting Malakor meant danger, but if what this boy said about his ship was true... and Malakor had wronged many in this very room.

Slowly, hesitantly, a few men detached from the crowd.

First, a wiry, quiet fellow named Finn. His eyes, usually downcast, now held a fierce, cold spark. "My village," he rasped, stepping forward, his hands, calloused from years of nets and hooks, clenching. "Malakor's men... they burned it. Took everything, everyone. I sailed out to fish and came back to ashes. I want his blood." Finn, once a simple fisherman, had been adrift in Tortuga for months, a shadow of his former self, consumed by a quiet, burning hatred for the man who'd destroyed his life. He saw an echo of his own loss in Xylar's eyes.

Next, a hulking, scarred brute known only as "Grog." He cared little for justice, and even less for sentimentality. His massive arms, adorned with faded tattoos, were folded across a barrel chest. "Revenge, justice, whatever. You speak of a ship that can outrun anything, that can take a beating? And a fight against Malakor?" He grinned, a flash of yellowed teeth. "Sounds like a good fight. Better than rotting in this tavern. I'm in for the chaos, lad. And the plunder, of course." Grog had a reputation for being a bruiser, loyal only to the prospect of violence and coin, but his sheer strength was undeniable.

Then, a lithe figure, surprisingly, emerged from the shadows near the back. Lyra, a quick-witted smuggler with a glint of mischief and danger in her sharp eyes. Her movements were fluid, predatory. "Malakor took a cargo from me once," she said, her voice a low, husky purr that nonetheless commanded attention. "A very valuable cargo. Cost me dearly with some unsavory types. And he did it just because he could. I've been waiting for a chance to pay him back, and this… this sounds like the kind of reckless idiocy I can get behind. Consider me your navigator, Captain. I know these waters better than any chart." Lyra had a network of contacts and an uncanny knack for finding hidden routes and evading pursuit, skills forged in years of clandestine trade. Her reasons were purely mercenary, yet she felt a flicker of grudging respect for Xylar's audacious plan.

Suddenly, two identical figures, looking so alike it made Xylar's Vydar-influenced logic briefly falter, detached themselves from the crowd. They were Jett and Reef, boisterous twins with matching grins and an almost uncanny way of finishing each other's sentences. "We heard 'fight Malakor'!" Jett exclaimed, nudging his brother. "And 'legendary ship'!" Reef chimed in, equally enthusiastic. "He sunk our cousin's fishing boat last month, just for sport," Jett continued, shrugging off the loss with a pirate's casualness. "Sounded boring until now," Reef finished, a mischievous glint in his eye. "We're in for the chaos, and whatever shiny bits we can grab!" Xylar stared at them, a faint frown creasing his brow as he tried to reconcile their identical appearances. The concept of two beings so utterly alike, yet distinct, was a curious anomaly to his mind, a fleeting distraction from the gravity of the moment.

They weren't the finest pirates Tortuga had to offer, not the most disciplined or the most renowned. They were a motley collection of the desperate, the greedy, the vengeful, and the reckless. But they were men (and one woman). And Xylar, against all odds, had a crew. The first step on his long path to vengeance was taken.

Chapter 13: Forging a New Family

With a motley crew assembled, each face a blend of desperation, curiosity, and a shared hunger for something beyond their usual squalor, Xylar felt a strange mix of apprehension and grim satisfaction. Leading them through the bustling docks, he felt their gazes, a mixture of awe and skepticism, as they first laid eyes on the Revenge of the Sea Serpent. She sat low in her secluded cove, her dark hull a stark, almost seamless expanse that drank in the morning light rather than reflecting it. Her lines were impossibly sleek, smoother, and more predatory than any vessel built by human hands, and her mast, unusually slender yet obviously robust, seemed to touch the clouds. There was a subtle, almost imperceptible hum that resonated from her depths, a deep thrumming beneath the timber that spoke of latent power.

"By the stars, Captain," Finn whispered, his usual quietness replaced by open wonder as he ran a tentative hand over the cool, dark wood of her side. "She's... different."

Grog simply grunted, his eyes wide as he took in the ship's sheer scale and unusual design. "Looks like she could eat a dozen frigates for breakfast," he muttered, a grin slowly spreading across his scarred face.

Lyra walked her fingers along the smooth railing, a rare, almost childlike curiosity in her sharp eyes. "No exposed rigging, no creaking timbers, no patched sails," she murmured, more to herself than to Xylar. "She looks like she grew from the ocean itself."

Even Jett and Reef, usually so quick with a jest, stood in uncharacteristic silence for a moment, their twin expressions mirroring a genuine, if fleeting, sense of wonder before they quickly moved to explore every nook and cranny. The concept of two beings so utterly alike, yet distinct, remained a curious anomaly to Xylar's Vydar-influenced mind, much like the strange, elegant curves of his vessel.

His sleek, dark ship then cut through the sun-dappled waters of Tortuga's harbor, slipping past other vessels like a phantom. The cheers and jeers from the docks faded, replaced by the rhythmic slap of waves against the hull. The initial days on the open sea, however, were less about grand vengeance and more about grinding, often comical, reality. Xylar quickly learned that being a captain meant wrangling a disparate collection of human personalities, each with their own quirks and stubbornness.

Finn, the wiry former fisherman, quickly proved invaluable. His quiet demeanor belied an uncanny knowledge of the sea—its moods, its currents, the subtle shifts in the wind that spoke volumes to him. He became Xylar's de facto First Mate, his calm presence a steady anchor amidst the burgeoning chaos. "Grog", the hulking brute, naturally gravitated to Master-at-Arms, his intimidating presence and surprising strength making him fiercely protective of the ship, and perhaps even more so, its rum stores. His booming laughter often echoed across the deck, a stark contrast to Finn's quiet efficiency. Lyra, the cunning former smuggler, with her quick wit and sharper tongue, became the ship's unofficial Quartermaster and chief negotiator. She valued freedom and coin above all else, but Xylar sensed a deeper loyalty beginning to stir within her. As for Jett and Reef, the identical twins, they were a whirlwind of energetic mischief, seemingly everywhere at once, their movements often mirroring each other with unsettling precision. Xylar found himself often doing a double-take, their existence a delightful, yet illogical, puzzle to his Vydar-influenced mind.

Xylar found himself navigating not just treacherous currents, but the even more unpredictable currents of human personalities. His initial, precise, Vydar-influenced commands, born of logic and efficiency, were met with blank stares. "Adjust sail vector to optimize photonic absorption at a 47-degree angle!" he might call out. Grog would scratch his head, a bewildered grunt rumbling in his chest. Lyra, quick to adapt, would shout a translation, her voice cutting through the confusion: "He means trim the jib, boys, the Captain's lookin' for speed!" Xylar learned quickly that the most elegant solution was useless if his crew couldn't understand it. He began to simplify his language, to observe their methods, and to adapt his commands to their understanding.

The first real test of their newfound, fragile cohesion came on the second day, a squall that erupted from a deceptively clear sky. Dark clouds boiled overhead, and the sea turned violent. Xylar instinctively barked commands born of his alien knowledge: "Deploy aft stabilizers! Engage primary inertial dampeners!" He saw the momentary confusion on their faces, but the training he'd given them, rudimentary as it was, kicked in. Grog, his face grim, grappled with ropes, confused by the words but understanding the urgency. Lyra, her eyes narrowed against the driving rain, yelled, "Batten down the hatches, you dolts! Secure everything loose!" And Finn, placing an almost blind trust in Xylar, moved with practiced ease, securing loose equipment and checking lines. The Revenge of the Sea Serpent, despite the crew's frantic, improvised efforts, rode the squall with an uncanny ease, gliding over waves that should have swamped them, weathering gusts that would have shredded lesser sails. When the squall passed as abruptly as it began, leaving behind only choppy seas and a shimmering sky, the crew stared first at the ship, then at Xylar, with a mixture of bewilderment and profound respect. "By the depths," Grog grunted, wiping rain from his beard, "this ship really is a ghost. Never seen a vessel take a beating like that." Xylar simply nodded, a tight smile on his lips, learning that showing results was far more effective than any explanation, especially when those explanations risked revealing too much.

Playful antics, surprisingly, became their strange team-building. One evening, Lyra, perched on a coil of rope, challenged Xylar to "truth or dare." Choosing "truth," Xylar, ever vigilant to hide his alien origins, deadpanned, "I once knew a man who could eat a whole coconut, shell and all, in one bite. Said he was from… the high mountains." Grog roared with laughter, slapping his thigh. "Aye, I knew a fellow like that, lad! Big as an ox, he was!" The crew swapped exaggerated tales of impossible feats and outlandish characters, Xylar carefully weaving in plausible, yet undeniably impossible, details from his own experience, making his lies entertaining rather than suspicious. The twins, Jett and Reef, took to mimicking his expressions and movements, a subtle, often humorous, game that both annoyed and amused Xylar and further reinforced his quiet fascination with their duality.

A few days later, a near-disaster occurred when Grog, in a burst of enthusiasm during a deck-swabbing session, accidentally put his enormous foot through a section of the main deck, revealing the dark, impossibly smooth alien metal beneath. "What in the blazes is this, Cap'n?" he grumbled, trying to pry the unyielding material with his fingers. Xylar,

without missing a beat, quickly fabricated. "Ah, yes, that's…
the ancient Atlantean hull plating," he said with an air of deep
mystery. "It shifts, you see. Changes in the sea's temper.
Magical, of course. Can't be damaged by mortal means." Grog,
after futile attempts to pull it up or even scratch it, simply
shrugged, grunting in grudging admiration. The incident only
deepened the crew's awe of the ship's "enchantment," further
solidifying the legend Xylar was carefully crafting.

Xylar, for his part, found himself not just commanding, but
observing, learning. He watched Finn's silent competence,
Grog's booming, uncomplicated loyalty, Lyra's sharp,
calculating mind, and the twins' unpredictable enthusiasm. He
began to delegate, relying on their individual strengths rather
than trying to do everything himself. One quiet night, under a
sky ablaze with unfamiliar constellations, Finn approached
Xylar at the helm. "Cap'n," he said, his voice low, "that was a
brave thing you did, takin' on Malakor. Most would just hide."
Xylar looked out at the vast, indifferent ocean, the stars above
like scattered gems. "She was my family, Finn," he replied, a
raw honesty in his tone. "Just as you are becoming now." Finn
simply nodded, a silent understanding passing between them.

The Revenge of the Sea Serpent hummed beneath their
feet, no longer untamed but a powerful, responsive extension
of their collective will. Xylar, the alien observer, was becoming

a captain, and his motley crew, against all odds, was slowly forging itself into a new, unconventional family.

Chapter 14: To Dead Man's Cove

With a full crew now on deck, the Revenge of the Sea Serpent was no longer a lone struggle for Xylar but a seamless extension of his will and theirs. The ship soared across the waves, her low, almost imperceptible hum a constant, comforting thrum beneath their feet. Finn's quiet competence ensured sails were trimmed with surgical precision, his eyes always scanning the horizon. Grog, a mountain of muscle, handled the heavy ropes with surprising speed, his booming laughs now interspersed with focused commands. Jett and Reef, the identical twins, were a whirlwind of energetic mischief, their synchronized antics providing a much-needed levity that Xylar, to his surprise, found himself occasionally appreciating.

Their immediate quest was clear: find Redtooth Malakor. Xylar had spent hours poring over old, fragmented charts, but Malakor was too elusive, too secretive. He rarely stayed in one place, preferring to strike from the shadows and vanish without a trace. It was Lyra, nimble and sharp-eyed, who provided their first tangible lead.

One evening, as Xylar studied the charts spread across the helm, Lyra leaned against the railing beside him, a knowing glint in her sharp eyes. "Captain, if you want to find a viper, you don't look in its last strike zone. You find someone who deals with vipers." She traced a finger across the chart to a notoriously dangerous stretch of water. "Dead Man's Cove."

Xylar looked at her, his brow furrowed. He knew the legends of Dead Man's Cove—a graveyard of ships, guarded by jagged reefs and unpredictable currents, rumored to be haunted by drowned sailors. "Why there?" he asked, a hint of skepticism in his voice. "Malakor's never been known to operate out of such a... permanent-looking base."

"And he hasn't," Lyra confirmed, a wry smile playing on her lips. "That's why it's perfect. Dead Man's Cove is too much trouble for most, even for the Navy. I used it myself, back in my smuggling days. There are plenty of hidden passages, caves, and a community of folks who simply don't want to be found. They trade in information as much as goods. I know a few people there. Old contacts. They might know something, or know someone who does, about Malakor's movements, his suppliers, or where he's planning his next strike." Her words carried conviction; she clearly knew the treacherous waters and their inhabitants better than any chart could describe.

The crew, having overheard, exchanged nervous glances. Hunting Malakor was one thing; sailing into Dead Man's Cove was another. It was a death wish whispered among the most hardened buccaneers. But Lyra's confidence, combined with Xylar's unwavering resolve, seemed to quell their doubts. The information was vague, a whisper in the wind, but it was enough. It was a starting point, a thread to follow into the labyrinth. Xylar felt a surge of grim determination. Malakor's arrogance would be his undoing, but only if they could first find his scent. The Revenge of the Sea Serpent altered course, her bow now cutting directly towards the perilous waters of Dead Man's Cove.

The journey to Dead Man's Cove was swift, the Revenge of the Sea Serpent slicing through the waves with impossible grace. Days at sea settled into a rhythm, the hum of the ship's unique systems becoming a backdrop to their shared purpose. Xylar, still finding his footing as a leader of humans, spent hours on deck. He observed Finn meticulously checking the rigging, learning the subtle nuances of human navigation from the former fisherman's keen instincts. He watched Grog oversee the daily drills with booming commands, turning the haphazard movements of the crew into something resembling disciplined action. Lyra, ever restless, wove through the crew, her sharp ears gathering gossip and keeping morale, in her own wry way, afloat.

As they approached Dead Man's Cove, the air grew heavy with the scent of salt and damp stone. Jagged, black teeth of rock clawed at the sky, guarding the narrow, treacherous inlet. Lyra moved to Xylar's side at the helm, her usual mischievous glint replaced by a serious focus. "Alright, Cap'n," she said, her voice dropping to a low, warning tone. "This ain't no Port Royal. These folks are private. Smugglers, freebooters, and those who simply don't want to be found. Keep your questions sharp, your words few, and your hand ready. Let me do the talking." With an expert hand, she took the lead, guiding the Revenge of the Sea Serpent through the winding, perilous passage. The ship, with its dark hull and silent, slipped through the treacherous channel like a shadow, a ghost gliding past the skeletal remains of less fortunate vessels that littered the jagged shoreline. They were here, at the threshold of information, waiting to see what secrets Dead Man's Cove would yield.

Chapter 15: Whispers in Dead Man's Cove

The den was a huddle of ramshackle shacks clinging to the rocky shore, built from driftwood and salvaged timber. Wary figures, hardened by years of clandestine life, emerged from doorways and shadows as the sleek, unfamiliar vessel drew closer. Their eyes, though cautious, held a flicker of grudging curiosity for the Revenge of the Sea Serpent, now anchored quietly in the narrow inlet. Lyra, with a casual grace born of long familiarity, descended the gangplank first. She moved among them with an ease that belied the tension in the air, a confident sway to her hips that spoke of a history shared in this secretive place.

"Lyra!" A grizzled old man, his face a roadmap of wrinkles and scars, croaked from the porch of a tilting shack. "Heard you'd gone respectable! What brings a fancy ship like that back to our humble hideaway?" His gaze lingered on the Revenge of the Sea Serpent, a mixture of awe and suspicion in his eyes.

Lyra flashed him a wide, easy grin, one that reached her sharp eyes but held a hint of her usual cunning. "Respectability wore thin, Old Man Tiber. Too many rules, not enough rum." She gestured back to Xylar, who stood poised on the deck, observing. "Got myself a new captain, though. Young fellow. And he's got a mighty thirst for vengeance." She let the word hang in the air, allowing it to resonate with the shared grievances of the Cove's inhabitants.

Inside the largest shack, which served as a communal tavern, the air was thick with the pungent aroma of pipe smoke and cheap rum. The low hum of conversation died as Xylar and Lyra entered. Lyra, ever the master of a room, quickly broke the tension. With a flourish, she spun a captivating tale of the Revenge of the Sea Serpent being a salvaged marvel, touched by strange, ancient magics, its hull impenetrable, its speed unmatched. Its captain, she explained, was a driven youth, touched by tragedy, seeking a score against the one man who deserved it: Redtooth Malakor.

Over mugs of fiery rum, passed around freely by Lyra's insistence, the smugglers slowly loosened their tongues. They spoke of The Black Kraken, Malakor's infamous ship, but not in the ways Xylar had expected. "Came upon us just a few weeks back, out near the Serpent's Tooth," Kael, a gaunt smuggler with haunted eyes, muttered, clutching his mug. "Thought we were dead men, for sure. He was chasing something, fast. But then… another ship, a fat merchantman, strayed too close. Malakor's cannons turned on them. We slipped away in the chaos." Kael shuddered, his voice dropping to a whisper. "Saw 'em… saw 'em burn. Just like the Sea

Serpent." He glanced at Xylar, a shared understanding of horror passing between them.

Another smuggler, Lena, a stout woman with a grim set to her jaw, nodded fiercely. "Leaves one survivor, always. To spread the word. To keep the fear alive." Her eyes, sharp and knowing, met Xylar's, acknowledging the grim fraternity they now shared.

The smugglers offered little concrete information on Malakor's immediate hideout. "Never stays in one place," Lena warned, swirling the rum in her mug. "Moves like a shark, striking then gone. No one here knows where he berths his ship for long, not truly." But they provided fresh water, salted meat, dried fruit, and plenty more rum – a sign of their cautious acceptance. And a vague direction: "Whispers of raids recently, further north than usual, near the Shifting Isles. Some new target he's got his eye on, something big. Malakor's shadow might be long enough to stretch that far." It wasn't the precise location Xylar craved, but it was a starting point, a new vector to follow. The hunt was far from over, but the Revenge of the Sea Serpent now had a direction.

Chapter 16: Lyra's Labyrinth: A Smuggler's Heart

Leaving the secretive confines of Dead Man's Cove behind, the Revenge of the Sea Serpent sliced through the waves, guided by the vague directions towards the Shifting Isles and, more importantly, Lyra's intimate knowledge of the treacherous northern waters. The intel from the Cove was thin, merely whispers of Malakor's recent, unusual activities further north, but it was a trail, however faint.

Days turned into nights, the rhythmic hum of the ship a constant companion. As Xylar plotted their course, observing Lyra's almost instinctive command of the unpredictable currents, he couldn't help but be impressed. "You seem to know these hidden routes like the back of your hand, Lyra," he observed one evening, the wind whipping strands of her dark hair across her face.

Lyra shrugged, a casual gesture that belied the depth of her past. "Been sailing these waters since I was old enough to hold a lantern, Cap'n. My family they were… collectors. Of things that people preferred to keep quiet about." Her voice, usually sharp and witty, softened, a rare glimpse into a hidden vulnerability. She spoke of scuttling through moonlit coves, the thrill of evading patrols, the constant tension of dodging both Navy ships and rival crews eager to snatch their illicit gains. "It was a labyrinth, these northern routes. Every island is a potential hideout, every tide a new challenge. We learned to blend with the shadows, to move where no one expected."

"Why leave that life?" Xylar asked, his Vydar-influenced mind seeking the logical shift in her life's trajectory.

Lyra paused, her gaze distant, fixed on the shimmering horizon. "Got tired of running, mostly. Always looking over your shoulder. And Elara… she offered something different. A purpose beyond just the next score, a crew that felt like… a real family. A fool's dream, perhaps, but it was a dream I was willing to chase." She took a deep breath, her voice hardening. "And Malakor… he tried to 'recruit' me once. Said I was too clever to be free, that I belonged in his collection of tools. I escaped, but it cost me. I don't forget debts, Cap'n. Not ever." This was Lyra's personal stake in their hunt, a quiet, festering wound that ran deeper than mere coin or convenience.

Her skills, honed in that dangerous life, were indispensable. During a tense encounter with a heavily armed naval patrol, it was Lyra who, with lightning-quick thinking and a silver tongue, concocted a convincing story of being a distressed merchant vessel, lost and struggling after a phantom squall. While Xylar, hidden at the helm, piloted the Revenge through daring, precise maneuvers that astonished even Lyra, she stood at the rail, weeping crocodile tears and spinning a tale of woe so convincing it brought a lump to Finn's throat. The patrol, bored and unsuspecting, eventually let them pass with a condescending wave. "That, Cap'n," she said later, wiping her eyes with a theatrical flourish, "is how you fight without drawing steel. A well-placed lie is sometimes more potent than a cannonball." Xylar, ever the pragmatist, meticulously logged the effectiveness of "emotional manipulation" and theatrical performance as tactical tools.

Lyra also became Xylar's unexpected tutor in human social currents. "You got a good ship, Cap'n," she advised one quiet afternoon as he struggled to understand a minor squabble between two crewmen. "And you know how to command. But these men... they ain't just automatons. They need to feel seen. Need to believe you're one of them, even when you're not." She taught him the art of a well-placed compliment, a shared joke, and feigned interest in their mundane stories. Under her shrewd guidance, Xylar slowly shed his alien awkwardness, developing a surprising, albeit calculated, charisma that began to bridge the gap between captain and crew.

The hunt for Malakor remained elusive, a frustrating chase across vast, empty stretches of ocean. Yet, with each passing day, the bond between Xylar and his motley crew deepened. Lyra, Finn, and Grog were more than shipmates; they were the pillars of his new, strange family, each playing a vital role in his transformation from a solitary survivor to a genuine leader.

Chapter 17: A Graveyard of Ships

Days blurred into a seamless tapestry of sea and sky as the Revenge of the Sea Serpent cut through the northern waters towards the vague promise of the Shifting Isles. Then, one hazy morning, a pall of black smoke, thick and acrid, smudged the horizon. It wasn't the distant haze of a cooking fire, but something vast and terrible. As the Revenge surged closer, propelled by Xylar's silent command, a horrifying tableau of destruction unfolded. The smell of burnt timber and gunpowder stung the air, clinging to their clothes and hair, a stench of death and ruin. The ocean was a dark, churning mess of debris – splintered planks, tattered sails, shattered masts, and the grim, unmistakable flotsam of a battle fought to the bitter end. Three, perhaps four ships, were burning hulks, their charred ribs reaching like skeletal fingers towards the indifferent sky. It was the aftermath of a mighty, brutal battle, fresh and devastating.

"By the depths!" Grog rumbled, his voice low with a mix of awe and grim recognition. His usual boisterous demeanor was replaced by a somber stillness. "Looks like Malakor's been busy." His hand instinctively went to the hilt of his cutlass.

Among the wreckage, clinging precariously to the remains of a capsized dinghy, was a lone figure. His face was streaked with soot and blood, his clothes torn and waterlogged, but incredibly, he was alive. "A survivor!" Lyra exclaimed, her sharp eyes spotting him first. Xylar, a cold knot tightening in his gut, ordered the Revenge to approach cautiously. The ship glided silently through the debris field, a dark angel amidst the devastation. Grog was the first to reach out, his massive hand extending to the shivering man. With a grunt of effort, he hauled the soaked figure aboard.

As the survivor collapsed onto the deck, shivering violently, Grog froze. His usually gruff face softened, then twisted with disbelief. "Rory?! By all that's holy, Rory, is that truly you?!" The survivor, a wiry man with bright red hair now matted with grime, blinked slowly, his eyes trying to focus. A weak, almost disbelieving smile touched his lips. "Grog? You old sea dog!" The two men, a hulking brute and a bedraggled waif, embraced, a rare moment of raw emotion on the blood-soaked deck. Rory, it turned out, was an old sailing companion of Grog's, from before Grog's pirate days, a bond forged in earlier, simpler times.

Rory was quickly given a blanket, strong rum to warm his core, and hot stew to fill his empty belly. While he ate, the crew gathered, a silent, grim audience, their curiosity tempered by the scene of carnage around them. After he had eaten and rested, the tremor in his hands slowly subsiding, he began to speak, his gaze distant, lost in the horror he had witnessed.

"We were on a trade run," Rory began, his voice hoarse but steadying. "Captain 'Lucky' Jack, God rest his soul, he thought we had a clear passage. Three ships we were, laden with spices and silks." He paused, taking a ragged breath, the memory clearly tormenting him. "Then it came. Out of nowhere. The Black Kraken. That monstrous black ship, silent as death, faster than anything on the waves. Malakor's flag unfurled... a sight that curdles your blood and freezes the very air."

Rory's eyes took on a glazed, haunted look, reflecting the inferno he'd escaped. "Malakor didn't even hail us. No demands for surrender, no parley. Just cannons blazing. So precise, so utterly merciless. They took down The Golden Gull first, her mast splintering like kindling. Then they boarded, like a swarm of demons, screaming and laughing. No quarter given. Just... slaughter. My friends, good men... they were cut down like dogs. We tried to fight, but there were too many. Too fast. Too... vicious. Malakor's men moved with a cold, practiced efficiency that wasn't human."

"My ship, The Wandering Star... we fought 'em hard," Rory said, his voice laced with pride and grief. "Stood our ground as long as we could. But Malakor himself boarded us. A towering shadow. He moved like a phantom, quick as a striking snake." Rory shuddered, a full-body tremor this time. "He killed Jack with his own hand. Just laughed as the life drained from his eyes. And then he looked right at me, Cap'n. Right into my soul. Said, 'Tell them what you saw. Tell them Redtooth Malakor never leaves a warning unheard. Tell them what happens to those who stand in my way.' He wanted a survivor. He wanted the terror to spread."

Rory's tale hung heavy in the smoke-filled air, a chilling testament to Malakor's calculated brutality. For Xylar, it was a new, horrifying piece of the puzzle. "The Shifting Isles," he murmured, his gaze falling upon the devastated wreckage around them. This attack wasn't random; it was a continuation of Malakor's recent movements, a brutal, deliberate message aimed at spreading fear and asserting dominance in these northern waters. The hunt had received its first bloody, undeniable clue, confirming their direction and deepening the personal vendetta that drove them all.

Chapter 18: A Town Aflame with Gossip

With Rory now a grim, gaunt addition to their motley crew, his presence a stark, living testament to Malakor's cruelty, the Revenge of the Sea Serpent charted a course northeast towards the treacherous Shifting Isles. Days at sea blurred, a relentless pursuit across the vast, indifferent ocean, allowing for a deeper, quieter forging of the crew. Rory often found himself by Grog's side, the two old companions sharing hushed words, their voices sometimes thick with forgotten memories, sometimes low with the fresh trauma of Rory's escape. Grog's protective instincts, usually reserved for the ship and its rum, now clearly extended to his red-haired friend. Finn, ever the silent observer, watched these interactions, his own quietude holding a hidden world of pain.

One evening, as the sun dipped below the horizon, painting the sky in fiery hues that mirrored the anger in his heart, Finn found himself at the ship's bow, staring out at the endless expanse. Xylar, sensing the depth of his unspoken thoughts, joined him. The silence between them was heavy, filled with the echo of Rory's tale and the lingering scent of smoke.

"Hard to look at all this," Finn murmured, his voice rough, gesturing vaguely towards the distant, darkening horizon where Malakor's shadow still loomed. "And not remember what it took from you." His hands, usually so adept with lines and sails, clenched into tight fists.

"Malakor," Xylar stated, his voice flat, a name that carried the weight of everything they had lost.

Finn's jaw tightened, a muscle twitching in his cheek. "Aye, Malakor. He didn't just sink a ship, Cap'n. He came to my village. Not a bustling port like Tortuga, just a small fishing village nestled in a quiet bay. Generations lived there, simple folk. We had no wealth for him to steal, no great ships to board. They burned it. Every hut, every boat. Just because it pleased them. Left us with nothing but ashes and the smell of burnt flesh." His eyes, usually serene like the deepest parts of the ocean, now held a cold, burning rage. "My family... I was out on the fishing boat, just a boy then, learning the nets. Came back to smoke. To silence. To bodies floating in the tide. My parents... my sister... gone. All gone, because of his casual cruelty. I've lived for nothing but the taste of his comeuppance since that day." He paused, taking a ragged breath, the words tearing from him. "That's why I'm here now, Cap'n. It ain't just your fight. It's ours. All of us." Xylar felt a strange, cold kinship with Finn, a shared, profound emptiness born of Malakor's senseless destruction. Their individual fires of vengeance now merged into a collective inferno.

After several more days of relentless sailing, pushing the Revenge to impossible speeds that would have shattered any other vessel, a small, bustling port town appeared on the horizon, nestled against a backdrop of rolling hills. It was a necessary stop; supplies were dwindling, and their fresh water was dangerously low. Lyra, ever resourceful, expertly guided them into a less-frequented dock, away from the main harbor traffic. Still, the Revenge, with its sleek, dark hull and unnerving silence, drew curious stares. Whispers began to ripple from the moment their gangplank touched the weathered planks. "The Ghost Ship," some called it, their voices hushed. "Came out of nowhere..."

The crew scattered, eager for solid ground and a change of scenery. Xylar, Finn, Grog, Lyra, and Rory headed for the "Kraken's Embrace" tavern, a place that promised strong drink and loose tongues. As they ate a hearty meal of salt pork and hardtack, Xylar, now more attuned to human nuances thanks to Lyra's lessons, noticed subtle shifts in conversation around them. Hushed tones. Nervous glances in their direction. The usual boisterous chatter was strangely subdued, replaced by an undercurrent of unease.

A red-faced sailor, clearly emboldened by too much ale, stumbled over to their table, his eyes wide and bloodshot. "You lot... you're with the Revenge, aye? Heard tales... huntin'

Malakor." He whispered loudly, his breath smelling of rum: "Bad news, lad. Word's out. Redtooth… he's caught wind of ya. Heard he's dispatched some of his own men. His top hunters. To come and find you. He knows you're comin' for him." The man swayed back, his drunken revelation hanging heavily in the smoky air.

The crew exchanged worried glances. This was a dangerous escalation. Rory swallowed hard, his face paling even further. Grog's hand instinctively went to the knife at his belt, his knuckles white. Finn's face was grim, his eyes burning with renewed fury. Xylar, however, felt a strange, cold calm settle over him. A surge of righteous fury burned through him, refining his focus. He set his tankard down with a decisive thud that echoed in the sudden silence of their corner of the tavern. He looked at his crew, then out at the uneasy faces in the tavern, letting his voice carry, low but clear, cutting through the tension. "So be it," he declared. "He thinks he can hunt us? Let him try. This isn't just a chase anymore, it's a challenge. A declaration of war." He rose, his youthful face set with an unyielding determination, his posture radiating a quiet power. "Let him send his best. Let him send his worst. I will not stop. I will not rest. I will not cease hunting Redtooth Malakor until the day I die. And if I fall," he added, looking directly at Finn, Lyra, and Grog, his gaze unwavering, "then one of you will pick up the hunt. Malakor will pay. No matter the cost. No matter what." A ripple went through the tavern, a mix of fear and stunned admiration. The declaration was bold, reckless, and brave. A grim, shared determination settled on his crew's faces. The hunt had become personal for the hunter as well, a war declared on the waves.

Leaving the hushed, nervous atmosphere of the Kraken's Embrace, Xylar and his crew made their way back through the dimly lit streets towards the docks. The air was cooler, the sea breeze a welcome respite from the smoky tavern. They moved with purpose, the weight of Xylar's declaration settling into a quiet resolve among them. As they approached the more secluded dock where the Revenge of the Sea Serpent lay, a lone figure detached himself from the shadows near a stack of crates. He was a wizened old wharf rat, his face a web of sun-creased wrinkles, clutching a fishing net. He looked them over with eyes that had seen too much, then fixed on Xylar.

"Heard your grand pronouncement, young captain," the old man rasped, his voice gravelly. "Bold words, indeed. Malakor's a beast that doesn't just lurk in the shadows of the Shifting Isles. There's talk he's made his true lair in the very heart of them, on a place they call Fiery Peaks." He leaned closer, his voice dropping to a conspiratorial whisper. "An active volcano, they say. A fortress carved into the rock itself, where the very earth bleeds fire. No one dares go near it, not unless Malakor calls them." He nodded towards the northern horizon. "If you truly want to find the beast, that's where you'll find his den. A place of fire and shadows." With that, the old man shuffled away, melting back into the darkness before Xylar could question him further.

Xylar turned to his crew, the grim set of his jaw illuminated by the pale moonlight. The Shifting Isles were vast, but this was a specific, terrifying location. The Fiery Peaks. A volcano, a true lair for a monster. A final, decisive destination. Without a word, they boarded the Revenge, the ship's silent hum a cold promise in the night. The hunt was no longer just a hunt; it was a pilgrimage to a monster's forge.

Chapter 19: Approaching the Beast's Lair

The intelligence from the old wharf rat at the docks of the small port town had solidified their purpose. Fiery Peaks. An active volcano, a fortress carved into the very stone. This wasn't just a hideout; it was a defiant declaration from Malakor. As they slipped back onto the Revenge of the Sea Serpent under the cloak of night, the hum of the ship's core felt less like comfort and more like a coiled spring, ready to unleash.

The next day and a half were spent in a tense, meticulous preparation for what everyone knew would be the ultimate confrontation. The Revenge sliced through the waves, her impossible speed eating up the distance to the Fiery Peaks with unnerving efficiency. Xylar ordered a full inspection of the ship's systems, ensuring everything was operating at peak performance. He worked silently, methodically, his Vydar focus a stark contrast to the human anxieties simmering around him.

Grog, ever the pragmatist, oversaw the armaments. Cutlasses were sharpened until they gleamed like hungry mirrors, pistols were meticulously cleaned and loaded, and the ship's complement of grappling hooks and boarding axes were laid out for easy access. He moved among the crew, his booming voice quieter than usual, offering gruff encouragement and reminding them of drills they'd practiced countless times. "Keep your wits, lads! And your powder is dry! Malakor's curse fight dirty, but we fight for something!"

Finn, his face grim, kept a vigilant watch, his eyes constantly sweeping the horizon, not just for the destination, but for any sign of Malakor's hunters that the drunken sailor had warned them about. He double-checked the rigging, anticipating every possible maneuver Xylar might call for, his quiet efficiency a balm to the growing tension. He ran through mental scenarios, calculating wind and current, imagining evasive actions. The quiet rage that now fueled him made him sharper, more focused.

Lyra, ever the realist, moved through the ship, her keen eyes assessing the crew's morale. She distributed the remaining rum sparingly, a swig for courage, not for drunkenness. She spoke in low tones with her shipmates, offering a wry joke here, a shared grim nod there, ensuring they understood the gravity of their mission but didn't succumb to fear. She meticulously reviewed the charts of the Shifting Isles again, trying to predict entry points and escape routes from a volcanic caldera, a task she knew was almost impossible. Rory, still gaunt but recovering, huddled with the other crew, listening intently to Lyra's words, his quiet presence a constant reminder of what they were fighting against.

Xylar, for his part, tried to impart the basics of the Revenge's unique capabilities to his key crew, should the unthinkable happen. He simplified the concepts, relying on analogies and brute memorization rather than true understanding. "This lever," he told Lyra, pointing to a control panel, "controls the ship's surge of speed or quick change of direction. Push it quickly, repeatedly, in rapid succession." He demonstrated, his hand a blur. Lyra nodded, her eyes wide with curiosity at the ship's strange magic. He spent time with Finn, explaining how the Revenge could hold impossible courses against the wind, almost as if willing itself forward against the very elements. He even showed Grog the ship's reinforced hull, demonstrating its resilience against direct impact, a fact that brought a rare, impressed grunt from the giant. He needed them to instinctively trust the ship's strange enchantments, even if they didn't understand its secrets.

As the second day drew to a close, a menacing, dark smudge began to appear on the horizon, growing steadily larger against the bruised, twilight sky. It was the jagged, volcanic silhouette of the Fiery Peaks, its craggy contours becoming sharply defined. A faint, metallic scent of sulfur, carried on the whipping wind, hinted at the distant, smoking caldera. The air itself seemed to grow heavy with anticipation.

Xylar ascended to the crow's nest, the familiar surge of purpose overriding any lingering human anxieties. His enhanced vision, now a crucial asset, immediately pierced the hazy distance. He scanned the labyrinthine coves and hidden inlets carved deep into the island's volcanic rock, the details sharpening into terrifying clarity.

And then, with a jolt that vibrated through his very core, he found it. Tucked deep within a vast, natural caldera that had formed an almost perfectly circular inner harbor, rested the black, menacing leviathan itself: The Black Kraken. Its three dark masts stood impossibly tall, its black sails, currently furled, hinting at terrifying speed. The ship exuded an aura of predatory power, even at rest.

But the Black Kraken was not alone. The inner harbor was a veritable viper's nest. Clustered around the flagship were at least a dozen other vessels. Smaller, certainly, but formidable: fast sloops, sturdy brigs, and heavily armed cutters, all flying variations of Malakor's grim flag. These were the ships of his henchmen, now forming a dense, unyielding guard. And beyond them, crowning the highest, most defensible peak, stood a grand, ominous castle, its dark stone walls seeming to rise organically from the volcanic rock, black as dried blood. This was it. Redtooth's lair. His fortress.

A cold, analytical calm settled over Xylar. This wouldn't be a simple skirmish. This was an assault on a pirate kingdom. He descended from the crow's nest, his face grim but resolute. "It's here," he announced to his waiting crew, his voice steady, carrying over the hum of the ship. "The Kraken. And a nest of vipers surrounding it. Malakor's castle watches over them all." The battle was about to begin.

Chapter 20: One Last Feast

The grim pronouncement from Xylar in the crow's nest – Malakor's massive fortress, the Black Kraken surrounded by a viper's nest of ships, and his castle looming above – had settled like a heavy cloak over the Revenge of the Sea Serpent. The battle to come would be unlike any they had faced. As the sun dipped below the horizon, painting the sky in fiery streaks that mimicked the distant peaks of the Fiery Peaks, a heavy, expectant silence fell over the ship. The air grew cool, carrying the faint, metallic tang of sulfur. The only sounds were the creak of the ship's timbers, the gentle slap of waves against her hull, and the distant, unsettling rumble of the volcano. Every man stood ready, a living weapon. The time for preparation was drawing to a close.

It was then, in that moment of solemn quiet, that Grog's booming voice cut through the tension. "Alright, you scurvy dogs!" he roared, a forced joviality in his tone that barely masked the gravity of the moment. "Cap'n says we eat! And by the Kraken's beard, we eat well! Tonight, we feast as a crew!"

Below deck, the ship's mess hall was transformed. Candles, usually conserved, flickered, casting dancing shadows on the rough-hewn walls. The last of the salted meats, the freshest bread painstakingly preserved, and every precious drop of rum were brought out from the stores. They gathered, a motley collection forged by fate and vengeance: Finn's quiet strength a solid anchor, Lyra's sharp wit a cutting edge, Grog's booming laughter a defiant rumble, Rory's haunted eyes reflecting past horrors, Stoke's stoic presence a steadfast resolve, and Pip's youthful enthusiasm a flicker of enduring hope.

They ate, and the rum flowed freely, warming their insides against the creeping chill of the night. Initially, the conversation was subdued, hesitant. But as the rum worked its magic, loosening tongues and lightening burdened hearts, the mood shifted. They talked of happier times, of wild escapades on distant shores, of drunken brawls in forgotten taverns, and improbable escapes from impossible odds. Finn, known for his stoicism, shared a rare chuckle about sailing his fishing boat by accident into a Royal Navy regatta, causing utter chaos. Lyra regaled them with a hilarious, almost unbelievable tale of haggling a pompous Duke out of his very breeches in a crooked card game. Even Stoke, usually silent and grim, offered a gruff smile at one of Grog's bawdy jokes, a rare crack in his hardened exterior. Pip absorbed every word, his young face alight with stories that would forever shape his understanding of these rough yet honorable pirates.

But as the night wore on, and the rum continued to flow, the conversation inevitably turned to the "bad times." To the ships they had lost, the friends they had buried, the dreams that had been shattered by the cruel hand of fate, or, more specifically, by Redtooth Malakor. Rory, his voice thick with unshed tears, spoke again of the Wandering Star and the chilling, triumphant laughter of Malakor as Captain Jack fell. Finn's face grew cold and distant as he remembered his village, reduced to ashes, and the haunting silence that followed. Lyra's usual bravado faltered, her gaze becoming shadowed as she recalled her own terrifying brush with Malakor's cruel "recruitment" attempts, a memory that still sent shivers down her spine.

The shared pain hung heavy in the air, a silent testament to the common enemy that bound them tighter than any blood oath. It was then that Xylar rose, his young form seeming to grow taller in the flickering candlelight, his presence commanding the room. "You have all suffered," he began, his voice low but clear, cutting through the somber quiet. "Malakor has taken something from each of us. He has tried to break us, to make us live in fear, to scatter us to the winds like ash. But he failed. He left one survivor, and that survivor found you. And together, we built something new. A ship born of vengeance, yes, but also of defiance. Of courage. We became a crew. A family. And tomorrow," he paused, his gaze sweeping over each of them, meeting their eyes with unwavering intensity, "this family sails into hell."

His gaze sharpened, becoming a cold, piercing light. "Tomorrow, we pay our respects to those we lost, not with tears, but with fire and steel. Tomorrow, we show Malakor what true terror looks like. Not the terror of a bully, of a man who takes what he wants, but the terror of those who have lost everything and have nothing left to lose. We are not just pirates. We are vengeance itself!"

"We sail for justice!" Xylar's voice rose, filling the mess hall, now a rallying cry. "We sail for every soul Malakor has ever wronged! We sail for the Revenge of the Sea Serpent!" He slammed his fist onto the table with a decisive thud. "In the morning, we unleash hell on those who have made us all suffer! For Elara! For our fallen! For the dreaded Redtooth!"

A guttural, unified roar erupted from the crew. Tankards crashed together, echoing the clash of swords and the thunder of cannons to come. Shouts of "For Elara!" and "For Revenge!" reverberated through the night. The fear was still there, a cold knot in their stomachs, but it was now overshadowed by a burning, collective fury. The feast ended not with quiet goodbyes, but with a unified roar of defiance, a promise whispered on the winds to the towering peaks ahead. In the morning, Malakor would learn the true meaning of a reckoning.

Chapter 21: A Captain's Vigil Under Alien Stars

The last echoes of the crew's defiant cheers from the mess hall had faded, replaced by the rhythmic creak of the ship and the soft murmur of the waves against its hull. The One Last Feast had done its work, forging a unified, if somber, resolve. Below deck, the Revenge of the Sea Serpent was now silent, its crew finally finding what rest they could before the coming storm, before the reckoning they had sworn to unleash. Xylar, however, found no such peace. The weight of his oath, the burden of his newfound human emotions, held him captive.

He walked the length of his dark ship, a lone, brooding figure, his steps soft, almost imperceptible against the hum of the alien technology that permeated the vessel. The air was cool, carrying the familiar tang of salt and the faint, unsettling scent of sulfur from the looming, volcanic island that now dominated the horizon like a sleeping beast. He gazed up at the night sky, a canvas ablaze with countless stars, and for the first time in what felt like an eternity, his mind drifted far from the impending battle, back to a life that seemed impossibly distant.

He remembered a younger version of himself, not in this human form, but in his true, ethereal state. An orphaned kid on a vast, sterile colony world, raised by the benevolent but impersonal collective, yearning for something more than calculated data and predictable routines. He hadn't been an outcast, precisely, but an anomaly – a researcher whose quiet, analytical mind yearned for the vibrant, unpredictable chaos of uncontained life. He'd devoured historical simulations of ancient expeditions, dreamt of distant galaxies teeming with wild, untamed civilizations. He yearned to be part of something grand, something that hummed with a different kind of purpose than the cold, logical pursuit of knowledge. He had longed for adventure, for stories that weren't just data points on a screen, for a family that was not just a collective unit.

Project Terra, the seemingly straightforward observation mission to this vibrant, chaotic planet, had been his ticket. He had imagined a quiet, detached study, meticulously cataloging the curious behaviors of the "Human" species from a safe, academic distance. He had envisioned himself returning to his homeworld, a decorated scientist, with volumes of precise data on "Emotional Variance Factor" and "Social Bonding Metrics." The irony of his current predicament was a bitter taste in his unfamiliar human mouth.

Now, under these same alien stars, he pondered the stark, almost surreal divergence of his path. What started as a simple, objective observation mission for a young, aspiring scientist had not just blossomed, but exploded, into a wild, unpredictable saga of desperate survival, profound loss, visceral murder, and an all-consuming thirst for revenge. He questioned every decision, every improbable turn that had led him to this precipice. Was this the right path? Was he truly doing justice to the memory of Elara and the Sea Serpent crew by embracing the very human chaos and violence he was meant to merely observe? His original self, the quiet, analytical youth driven by pure scientific curiosity, seemed like a ghost from another lifetime, lost in the shadows of this new, hardened persona forged in fire and blood. He wondered if that past self would even recognize the vengeful captain he had become, standing on the deck of a warship born of sorrow.

The memories of the Sea Serpent crew flickered through his mind, not as abstract concepts, but as vibrant, aching presences: Elara's booming, infectious laughter that could chase away any storm, Grog's gruff good humor that masked a loyal heart, Finn's quiet wisdom that always seemed to cut to the core, Lyra's sharp wit that could disarm or disorient, the innocent excitement of Pip and the stoic resolve of Stoke. His first taste of rum, the dizzying thrill of a stormy sea, the inexplicable warmth of belonging, the feeling of being truly seen for the first time. They weren't just data points now; they were vibrant, aching presences in his memory, a family forged in the unlikely fires of shared experience. And they were gone, victims of Redtooth Malakor. Their faces, their voices, their laughter, each a precious memory that fueled the inferno in his soul.

Just as the overwhelming weight of his transformation and the crushing tide of grief threatened to drown him, a soft voice cut through the stillness. "Can't sleep, Cap'n?"

Xylar snapped back to reality, startled. He hadn't heard her approach, a testament to her smuggler's stealth. Lyra stood a few feet away, a silhouette in the pale moonlight, her usually mischievous eyes now soft, reflective, filled with an understanding that transcended words. She held out a shared mug of rum, the offer a simple gesture of quiet companionship. It was a rare, soft moment of bonding and camaraderie, a silent understanding passing between them without need for explanation or forced conversation. She didn't ask what he was thinking, didn't pry into the turmoil she knew must be visible on his face in the moon's stark light. She simply offered presence, a shared vigil in the face of the unknown.

Xylar accepted the mug, his fingers brushing hers. The liquid burned warmly as it went down, a stark, fleeting contrast to the cold, unyielding resolution that filled him. He looked at Lyra, a flicker of gratitude in his eyes, before his gaze inevitably drifted back to the dark, volcanic silhouette of the island. It was a hulking beast slumbering before its bloody awakening.

He knew the path he had chosen, the path he was compelled to walk. He was no longer just Xylar, the orphaned researcher dreaming of adventure, nor just Xy, the peculiar castaway learning to be human. He was the vengeful captain of the Revenge of the Sea Serpent, a vessel born of loss and fueled by an oath. And in the morning, hell would dawn, and he would be ready to meet it.

Chapter 22: Dawn Breaks, Hell Unleashed

The morning sun, a colossal orb of fiery orange and molten gold, began its slow, deliberate ascent over the eastern horizon. Its light spilled across the vast expanse of the ocean, but as it rose higher, it seemed to settle directly behind the formidable bulk of the Fiery Peaks. The effect was striking, almost theatrical: a great ball of flames rising behind the island, casting it in a fearsome, silhouetted glory. Even nature, it seemed, knew that fire was going to rain today. The very air crackled with a charged anticipation, heavy with the scent of sulfur from the volcano and the metallic tang of impending conflict. A low, persistent rumble, deep within the volcanic heart of the island, vibrated through the very hull of the Revenge, a primal drumbeat signaling the start of something terrible and magnificent.

On the deck of the Revenge of the Sea Serpent, there was a quiet, grim efficiency. The crew, hardened by their shared resolve and Xylar's impassioned speech of the previous night, moved with a synchronized purpose that bordered on ritual. Swords, polished to a wicked gleam, were drawn from scabbards and tested with swift, practiced swings, the shing of steel a stark counterpoint to the ocean's murmur. Cannons, their formidable mechanisms now fully exposed, were loaded with meticulous care, the heavy cannonballs thudding home, their muzzles aimed squarely at the dark outline of the island. Sails, carefully unfurled, caught the first whispers of the morning breeze, snapping taut with a muffled crack, ready to propel them into the maw of battle.

Finn, ever vigilant, ran a final check of the rigging, his hands moving with the practiced ease of a craftsman. His eyes, though outwardly calm, held a fire that burned cold and steady as he scanned the horizon, searching for any ripple on the water that might betray an enemy's approach. Grog, a mountain of muscle and determination, moved among the men, offering a gruff word of encouragement here, a reassuring clap on the shoulder there. "Remember Malakor's laugh, lads!" he rumbled low, his voice a gravelly whisper meant only for those nearest. "Let that be your powder!" Lyra stood by the helm, her eyes scanning the treacherous waters ahead, her mind already charting complex evasive maneuvers through the unseen currents and the very real threat of incoming fire. Her hand rested on the polished wood, feeling the subtle vibrations of the ship, a silent conversation between captain and vessel.

A heavy silence descended, broken only by the groan of timbers and the distant calls of gulls. Each man stood at his station, a living statue carved from anticipation and steel. Hearts hammered a frantic rhythm against ribs, every sense heightened, every nerve stretched taut. They had prepared, they had sworn, and now, they waited.

Just as the sun crested the highest peak, painting the sky in a blinding blaze, a piercing cry split the stillness of the dawn, echoing across the water like a physical blow.

"Enemy ships inbound!"

The shout came from Pip, perched in the crow's nest, his young voice surprisingly clear despite the tension that gripped them all. He pointed with a trembling hand towards the narrow channel leading out of the inner harbor, a thin finger of terror cutting through the morning light. Sure enough, four dark shapes, smaller than The Black Kraken but undeniably hostile, were already making their way towards the open sea. Their sails, black as pitch, rapidly unfurled like hungry wings, catching the wind as they surged forward. These were Redtooth's goon ships, dispatched to deal with the audacious intruder before it could even reach the main stronghold. Malakor, it seemed, was not one to wait for a challenge to come to his doorstep. He intended to snuff out the spark of the Revenge before it could ignite his entire kingdom. The first volley was imminent.

Chapter 23: Battle at Dawn: The Revenge Unleashed

The silence on the Revenge of the Sea Serpent became a living thing, thick with anticipation, broken only by the creak of timbers and the distant calls of gulls. The four dark shapes, Malakor's goon ships, were surging towards them, black sails unfurled, intent on snuffing out the Revenge before it reached the main stronghold. Xylar, at the helm, felt a cold calm descend upon him, sharpening his senses to an almost unnatural degree.

"Lyra, evasive pattern Beta-7!" His voice, a blend of precision and urgency, cut through the air. "Stoke, target their lead ship, aim for the mast! Finn, full sails, give me speed!"

The enemy ships, operating as a coordinated pack, fanned out, attempting to encircle the Revenge. Their own cannons roared, sending plumes of smoke and iron shot churning through the water, leaving frothing white trails in their wake. But the Revenge was unlike anything they had ever encountered. Its powerful propulsion system, now fully unleashed, allowed it to dart and weave with impossible agility, a phantom on the waves, leaving their cannon fire trailing harmlessly in its wake.

"Too slow, you brutes!" Grog roared from the main deck, his voice a booming challenge, as a volley passed harmlessly over their heads, churning the water just beyond their bow. Rory, standing grim-faced beside him, reloaded a musket with practiced efficiency, his movements sharp despite his recent ordeal. Jett and Reef, the young twins, hustled below deck, ensuring powder was swiftly brought up for the next salvo, their usual playful banter replaced by focused urgency.

Xylar, his eyes fixed on the lead enemy ship, a brigantine flying a tattered skull-and-crossbones, gave the order. "Fire!"

The Revenge's cannons unleashed a devastating, synchronized barrage. There was no visible recoil, no plumes of smoke to obscure their vision. Instead, streaks of concentrated energy, visible as shimmering blurs, shot across the water. The lead brigantine shuddered violently as the blasts tore into its hull, not splintering wood, but leaving sections of its deck vaporized and glowing. A secondary blast, aimed with uncanny precision by Stoke, struck its main mast near the base. With a sickening crack, the mast groaned, then snapped, toppling with a crash of rigging and canvas, sending men tumbling into the churning water below.

"One down!" Pip cheered from the crow's nest, his fear momentarily forgotten in the thrill of battle, his small fist punching the air.

But the other three ships pressed their attack with renewed ferocity, their captains enraged by the loss. One, a nimble sloop, attempted to flank them, its crew screaming curses as they tried to get into a boarding position. "Lyra, hard to port! Grog, prepare the boarding deterrents!" Xylar commanded. The Revenge turned on a dime, her powerful engines roaring. As the sloop drew alongside, its grappling hooks flying through the air, it was met not with musket fire but with jets of superheated steam erupting from hidden vents along the Revenge's sleek hull. The steam scalded, blinding, and drove the attackers back, some screaming as they fell, flailing, into the sea. Rory let out a grim chuckle as one desperate pirate splashed down near their hull.

"Now, Stoke!" Xylar bellowed. The untouched starboard cannons unleashed another volley, tearing into the sloop's exposed flank. The smaller ship buckled, its hull groaning under the onslaught, then began to list heavily, rapidly taking on water. Its crew scrambled in terror to abandon ship, leaving it to sink in a trail of bubbles and debris.

Two down. The remaining two enemy ships, a brig and a cutter, exchanged nervous signals, their previous confidence shattered. They had expected a conventional fight, not this phantom ship that seemed to dance through their fire and strike with invisible force. They tried to converge, attempting a desperate pincer movement.

"Finn, prepare for ramming speed! But not with the hull!" Xylar ordered, a dangerous glint in his eye. "Grog, man the stern guns! Rory, assist him!"

As the brig closed in, anticipating a broadside, Xylar executed a daring maneuver. He brought the Revenge to a sudden, almost impossible halt, then surged forward again at an oblique angle, not to ram, but to bring his unique stern-mounted projector into play. The brig, caught completely off guard by the sudden deceleration, surged past them. As it did, a focused beam of pure energy erupted from the Revenge's stern, slicing through the brig's rudder and its lower stern section like a hot knife through butter. The ship instantly lost steerage, spinning wildly in circles, its crew screaming in panic as water poured into its vital organs. Grog and Rory, manning the stern guns, cheered as the brig was crippled.

The last cutter, witnessing the utter annihilation of its companions, hesitated, its bravado evaporating. Its captain, a seasoned brute, knew a losing battle when he saw one. He screamed orders to change course, to flee, to warn Malakor of this impossible, ghost-like foe. But it was too late.

"Finn, precise aiming!" Xylar commanded, his voice cold and unwavering. "A single shot. Mast."

The Revenge's final cannon, charged and ready, unleashed its blast. A blinding flash, and the energy bolt soared, unerringly, impacting the cutter's mainmast precisely at its base. The mast exploded into splinters, sending wood and rigging showering down on the deck. The cutter, crippled and helpless, drifted aimlessly, a broken bird on the water, its fight extinguished.

All four ships were dealt with. Smoke and steam billowed across the water, mingling with the acrid scent of burnt wood and the fading cries of the defeated. The Revenge of the Sea Serpent, untouched, glided through the wreckage, a dark, silent harbinger of doom. From the burning remains of Malakor's henchmen, the ship emerged from the smoke, sailing with the fury of all those scorned, a silent, unstoppable avenger. The fiery peaks of the island loomed larger, awaiting their inevitable visitor.

Chapter 24: Malakor's Counter: The Kraken Rises

The Revenge of the Sea Serpent cut through the last wisps of smoke from the crippled enemy ships, their fires slowly dying on the water. The earlier rush of triumph, sharp and intoxicating, began to recede, replaced by a cold knot of anticipation. The volcanic island, the Fiery Peaks, now loomed closer, its jagged summit silhouetted dramatically against the rising sun. Every man on deck knew the true challenge still lay ahead. The Revenge held her course, a lone, dark silhouette against the fiery dawn, sailing directly towards the vast, natural caldera that formed the island's inner harbor.

As the Revenge rounded a particularly large, smoke-shrouded outcropping of rock, the vast inner harbor of the volcano finally revealed itself. The sight instantly chilled the celebratory mood from moments before, snatching the breath from the lungs of even the most hardened sailors.

There, where Xylar had first spotted it from the crow's nest, the colossal, three-masted silhouette of The Black Kraken was no longer at rest. It filled the narrow mouth of the harbor, a monstrous, living shadow. Its vast, dark sails, previously furled tightly against its masts, were now unfurling with ominous purpose, catching the morning breeze like predatory wings about to enfold their prey. The ship, a true leviathan, began to move, slowly at first, then gaining momentum, its black hull cutting a silent, predatory path directly towards the open sea. Its deck bristled with armed men, a dark swarm of activity, figures moving with grim efficiency around the countless cannonports that lined its immense sides.

And behind it, accompanying their monstrous flagship like a grim, relentless escort, were Malakor's remaining goon ships. Xylar quickly counted them: eight vessels, a menacing mix of fast sloops, sturdy brigs, and heavily armed cutters, all painted in dark, foreboding colors and flying variations of the dreaded Kraken flag — some emblazoned with a bloodied tentacle, others with a gaping maw. They fanned out, forming a deadly crescent behind their lord's vessel. Redtooth Malakor, it seemed, had witnessed the destruction of his vanguard from his lair. He hadn't retreated, nor had he waited. He was taking the battle to them, personally, leading his entire, formidable fleet out from his volcanic den. The very air thrummed with the sheer audacity of his appearance, a challenge thundering across the waves that made the hairs on the back of every neck stand on end.

"Malakor!" Grog's voice, usually booming, was a low growl, laced with raw hatred, his knuckles white around the hilt of his cutlass. He braced his feet, his massive frame radiating defiance. Rory, standing beside him, gripped his own weapon, his eyes narrowed, remembering the horrors of the Wandering Star and the chilling laughter that accompanied its demise. A visible shiver ran through Pip, even from his position by the mast, as the black sails of the Kraken fully unfurled, blotting out a section of the sky.

"He's armed the Kraken!" Lyra exclaimed, her eyes wide as she saw the sheer number of remaining ships, each a dark shadow against the morning light, their combined might an overwhelming force. Her hand instinctively tightened on the helm, her mind racing, calculating odds that seemed impossible. Finn, at the rigging, tightened a final knot, his face grim, his gaze unwavering from the approaching fleet. Even Stoke, usually imperturbable, clenched his jaw as he began preparing the main cannons for the momentous clash. Jett and Reef exchanged nervous glances but continued to work with silent, practiced movements, securing every last piece of deck gear.

A grim resolve settled over Xylar. This was it. The true test. The culmination of everything that had brought him to this point, the weight of every lost life resting on his shoulders. He didn't hesitate. "Prepare for battle!" he roared, his voice resonating with an authority that left no room for doubt, cutting through the growing roar of the wind and the distant rumble of the volcano. "Stoke, ready the cannons! Finn, all hands to battle stations! Jett and Reef, secure the decks! This is for Elara! This is for the Sea Serpent! For every soul he's wronged!" The crew, their faces grim but determined, moved with a newfound fury to their positions, a unified force against the approaching storm, their roars echoing the challenge Malakor had thrown down, ready to face their reckoning.

Chapter 25: An Epic Engagement: Fury on the Waves

The silence on the Revenge of the Sea Serpent became a living thing, thick with anticipation, broken only by the creak of timbers and the distant calls of gulls. The eight dark shapes of Malakor's goon ships, a grim escort for the formidable Kraken, were surging towards them, black sails unfurled, intent on snuffing out the Revenge before it reached the main stronghold. Xylar, at the helm, felt a cold calm descend upon him, sharpening his senses to an almost unnatural degree.

"Lyra, evasive pattern Beta-7!" His voice, a blend of precision and urgency, cut through the air. "Stoke, target their lead ship, aim for the mast! Finn, full sails, give me speed!"

The eight enemy ships, operating as a coordinated pack, fanned out, attempting to overwhelm the Revenge with a complex, converging attack. Their own cannons roared, sending plumes of smoke and iron shot whistling through the air, leaving frothing white trails in their wake. But the Revenge was unlike anything they had ever encountered. Its powerful propulsion system, now fully unleashed, allowed it to dart and weave with impossible agility, a phantom on the waves. It would surge forward with blinding acceleration, abruptly swerve with a dizzying turn, or spin on its axis, leaving the enemy's cannon fire to harmlessly strike empty water or, sometimes, even other enemy ships caught in the confusion. The sea around them became a cauldron of near misses and frustrated splashes as Malakor's gunners struggled to track their elusive foe.

"They're hitting their own!" Pip cried out excitedly from the crow's nest, his voice shrill with a mixture of terror and glee, pointing as one of Malakor's sloops, attempting a desperate flanking maneuver, was suddenly caught in the furious crossfire of a clumsy brig, splintering its mast and sending men reeling. The swiftness of the Revenge and its uncanny ability to appear and disappear from view sowed confusion and panic among Malakor's less disciplined forces, their frustrated curses carried across the wind.

Xylar pressed the advantage, turning the enemy's chaos against them. "Stoke, target their rigging! Cripple them!" The Revenge's powerful cannons, deadly precise, spewed their glowing blasts. These were not mere cannonballs; they were focused lances of energy that cut through wood and rope with terrifying ease. Masts snapped with reports like thunderclaps, sails ignited in sudden, unnatural flares that lit up the pre-dawn gloom, and rudders were sheared away with surgical precision, leaving ships to spin helplessly. One by one, Malakor's ships fell. A brig, its sails in tatters and its hull smoking from deep scorch marks, began to list heavily, its crew scrambling like ants on a dying beast. A cutter, attempting a frantic turn to flee, found its stern blown apart by a devastating, silent shot, sending its aft section high into the air before it plunged into the depths.

Grog and Rory, manning the deck guns, cheered with savage delight as their shots found their marks, reloading with furious efficiency. "That's for Lucky Jack, you bilge rats!" Rory howled, his voice hoarse with adrenaline, as a cannonball from his side slammed into an enemy vessel's waterline, causing a fresh geyser of water to erupt. Jett and Reef, moving like shadows, darted across the deck, swiftly bringing up powder and shot, their small forms surprisingly resilient amidst the chaos, ducking instinctively as splinters flew past. The deck of the Revenge was a hive of controlled fury, every crew member performing their tasks with desperate precision, fueled by Xylar's grim leadership and their burning desire for retribution.

As the battle raged, Malakor, from the deck of The Black Kraken, watched with a cold, growing fury that threatened to erupt like the volcano itself. He barked orders, his voice carrying across the water, a frustrated roar, but even his seasoned crew seemed disoriented by the Revenge's impossible tactics. His ships were not just being defeated; they were being systematically dismantled, destroyed with an unnatural efficiency that defied all conventional naval warfare. He saw his lieutenants' vessels crippled, one after another, unable to land a significant blow on the dark, darting menace.

Finally, after what seemed an eternity, the last of Malakor's eight supporting vessels, a battered brig, was consumed by flames, its screams silenced by the hungry sea. The water around them was a graveyard of splinters, burning debris, and floating bodies. The grim cost of Malakor's hubris was etched into the churning waves.

The smoke began to clear, revealing the stark, awe-inspiring reality of the situation. An epic standoff had been achieved. In the vast, open expanse of the ocean, only two ships remained, utterly alone on the water, locked in a silent, deadly tableau.

On one side, the colossal, menacing silhouette of The Black Kraken, its dark hull scarred but intact, its cannons gleaming, Malakor himself a grim, towering figure at its helm, his rage a palpable force, his eyes fixed on his impossible adversary.

And on the other, the sleek, dark form of The Revenge of the Sea Serpent, untouched, hovering like a vengeful shadow, its guns still hot, a silent, deadly challenge thrown across the water.

The true battle had finally arrived.

Chapter 26: The Duel of Titans

The Revenge of the Sea Serpent, untouched and resolute, hovered like a vengeful shadow in the vast expanse of the ocean. Across the water, the colossal, menacing silhouette of The Black Kraken bristled, its cannons gleaming, Malakor a grim, towering figure at its helm. The air crackled with a palpable tension, a grim silence settling over the two titans locked in a deadly ballet as the sun, now higher in the sky, cast an unforgiving light upon them.

This was no mere pirate skirmish. This was a duel. A clash of wills, of unique power against brutal force, vengeance against tyranny.

Xylar, his gaze locked on The Black Kraken, felt an unnerving calm. He knew Malakor would not underestimate him again, having just witnessed the annihilation of his escort fleet. "They're faster than anything else out here, Cap'n," Lyra murmured from beside him, her usual bravado tinged with a rare caution. "And those cannons... they say they were forged in dragonfire, spitting hell itself."

"They will not be enough," Xylar stated, his voice a low hum of conviction, absolute in its certainty. "Finn, prepare for evasive maneuvers at my mark. Stoke, prioritize their cannon decks, cripple their firepower. Grog, ready for boarding deterrents, they'll try to overwhelm us if they get close." Rory stood ready at the closest deck cannon, his face a mask of fierce anticipation, while Jett and Reef moved swiftly below deck, ensuring powder and shot were constantly flowing to the gun crews.

Malakor, with a guttural roar that carried across the water, fired the first shot. A full broadside from The Black Kraken erupted, a terrifying wall of iron and flame that seemed to tear the very air. The sheer force of the volley was immense, far beyond any conventional ship, each cannonball a monstrous projectile. Xylar, anticipating the blast with uncanny foresight, had already begun his evasive sequence. The Revenge bucked and swayed, performing a maneuver that would have ripped a normal ship apart, a dizzying jink that left the Kraken's volley roaring harmlessly past. The shots screamed past, some dangerously close, sending geysers of water skyward where they struck, briefly obscuring the colossal enemy.

"They're faster than I anticipated!" Xylar acknowledged, a hint of surprise in his voice, not for himself, but for the ship. Malakor wasn't relying solely on brute force; he was using his flagship's surprising speed to his advantage, attempting to flank the Revenge with cunning ferocity.

The duel began in earnest. The Black Kraken, despite its immense size, moved with uncanny speed, circling the Revenge like a colossal predator, its cannons roaring incessantly, a relentless barrage of fire and smoke. It sought to find a weakness, to corner its agile foe. But the Revenge of the Sea Serpent danced, weaving through the chaos, its powerful engines humming a silent song of defiance. Xylar pushed the ship to its absolute limits, pulling off impossible turns, sudden decelerations that left chasing cannonballs far behind, and breathtaking accelerations that left Malakor's gunners bewildered, their aim constantly thrown.

"Aim for their waterline!" Malakor bellowed, his voice raw with fury as the Revenge slipped through yet another volley, seemingly untouched. "Blast them to the depths, you imbeciles!" His frustration was a palpable wave across the water.

Then, Xylar retaliated. "Stoke, open fire! Target their forward cannons!" The Revenge's powerful cannons spat their brilliant, silent blasts. Unlike cannonballs, these were focused energy, superheating and vaporizing targets with devastating precision. A series of explosions erupted along the Black Kraken's forward deck. Metal shrieked, wood turned to ash in sudden, searing flares, and chilling screams echoed across the water as several of Malakor's crew were caught in the inferno. A substantial section of The Black Kraken's main cannon battery was gone, ripped away as if by an invisible claw, leaving behind scorched, smoking ruin.

"They're taking hits, Cap'n!" Rory shouted, a grim satisfaction on his face, as he watched the destruction on the enemy vessel. His grin was sharp, reflecting the justice he had waited so long to see

Chapter 27: The First Major Blows

Rory's cheer, sharp with satisfaction, was swallowed almost immediately by the renewed roar of The Black Kraken's remaining cannons. Malakor, though having just seen his flagship crippled by the loss of its mainmast, was far from defeated. He was a veteran of countless battles, a brute of cunning, and The Black Kraken was a ship designed for war, capable of absorbing and delivering immense punishment. With a tactical shift that surprised even Xylar, Malakor altered his approach. Instead of wide, sweeping broadsides, he began to fire precise, concentrated salvos at The Revenge's main mast and rigging, aiming to cripple its maneuverability. He sought to pin down his elusive foe.

One particularly heavy volley struck home. A deafening roar tore through the air as three heavy cannonballs, seemingly aimed with uncanny malice, slammed into The Revenge's port side. The ship shuddered violently, a gut-wrenching tremor that threw men off their feet. Ship's bells clanged frantically through the chaos of battle, their urgent peals signaling immediate, severe damage below deck.

"Damage reports!" Xylar yelled, grabbing the helm to steady the bucking ship, his calm voice a stark counterpoint to the rising panic.

"Hull breach, port side, deck two!" Finn shouted, already sprinting towards the damage with a team, his movements a blur of practiced urgency. "And the main sail torn! We're losing speed!"

"Explosions!" Pip shrieked from the crow's nest, pointing to thick, acrid smoke billowing from below deck near the stern. "Something's hit the secondary power conduits!"

Chaos erupted on The Revenge's deck. The organized fury from moments before fractured into a scramble of desperate action. Men were running, shouting, and scrambling to assess and mitigate the damage. Fire started to spread near the compromised power conduits, forcing a frantic flurry of activity to contain it. Grog, roaring orders that cut through the alarm, directed crewmen with buckets of water, their desperate efforts a stark contrast to the ship's advanced nature. Stoke, cool under fire, directed teams to patch the hull breach with quick-drying composite materials Xylar had prepared for such emergencies. Jett and Reef, despite their young age, bravely joined the bucket brigade, their small faces smudged with soot, their efforts relentless as they battled the encroaching flames.

"She holds! She still holds!" Grog bellowed, even as he coughed on a lungful of smoke, his voice a testament to the ship's resilience.

Xylar gritted his teeth, a muscle ticking in his jaw. His magnificent ship, the culmination of his desperate efforts, was taking a brutal pounding. It was holding its own, far better than any normal vessel, its unique construction absorbing blows that would have splintered lesser ships. But Malakor's relentless, focused assault was indeed breaking through The Revenge's defenses, a testament to the Kraken captain's grim determination. Xylar's initial surprise at Malakor's resilience was growing into a grudging respect. The Black Kraken was truly a formidable foe, and its captain a relentless opponent.

"Lyra, evasive pattern Rho-9!" Xylar commanded, pushing the ship into another complex maneuver, trying to buy time for repairs, for his crew to contain the spreading damage. "Give them everything we have, Stoke! Target their deck batteries!"

The Revenge unleashed a furious counter-barrage, focusing its energy on The Black Kraken's formidable deck guns. More explosions ripped across the black ship's deck, showering it with debris, silencing several of its cannons, and sending plumes of black smoke skyward. The air vibrated with the continuous roar of artillery and the sickening crunch of impacts. Neither ship was gaining a decisive advantage; both were delivering and taking devastating blows in a brutal, tit-for-tat exchange of power and resilience. The outcome of the duel remained agonizingly uncertain.

Chapter 28: The Chaos Unravels: Malakor's Escape

The battle raged for what felt like an eternity, a relentless, deafening symphony of destruction. The Revenge of the Sea Serpent, battered but unbowed, continued to unleash its unique fury. Its experimental shields, though damaged by The Black Kraken's relentless assault, deflected countless shots, and its repairs were miraculously swift, thanks to Xylar's foresight and the resilient materials he had brought. Malakor, however, was equally relentless. He continued to exploit every perceived weakness, pushing The Black Kraken with savage intensity, matching Revenge's tenacity with his own brutal will. Explosions bloomed across the waves, a macabre fireworks display painting the dawn sky.

Xylar, monitoring the battle's ebb and flow with his sharp senses, realized that while they were inflicting heavy damage, Malakor's ship simply refused to break. The Black Kraken was tougher, more resilient than anything Xylar's calculations had predicted for a human-built vessel. Its very structure seemed to absorb impacts, its crew, driven by fear and loyalty to their monstrous captain, repairing damage with frenetic zeal, their shouts of defiance occasionally audible over the din.

Just as Xylar was about to initiate a desperate, high-risk maneuver to disable The Black Kraken's rudder—a move that would put The Revenge at significant risk—a thick, dark cloud of smoke, far denser than any battle had yet produced, began to billow from the volcanic island itself. It wasn't just ordinary smoke; it was acrid, choking, and incredibly dense, rolling out across the water like an ominous, living wall, seemingly summoned by the sheer intensity of the conflict.

Malakor, seeing his opportunity in the sudden, natural obscuration, seized it with the cunning of a cornered beast. Amidst the choking smoke and the lingering chaos of the battle, he barked a series of rapid, urgent commands. The Black Kraken, still formidable despite its wounds and its downed mainmast, suddenly changed course. Its powerful engines surged, making a desperate, powerful dash directly for the most treacherous, reef-laden passage leading back into the inner harbor of the Fiery Peaks.

"He's running for the caldera!" Lyra shouted, coughing in the sudden, thick smoke that billowed around them, instantly reducing visibility. "He's using the cover! We can't see a thing!"

Xylar pushed The Revenge forward, but the visibility had dropped to almost zero, a blinding shroud enveloping both ships. He could hear the faint, triumphant cackle of Malakor carried on the wind, mocking them. He could sense the Black

Kraken's powerful engines pushing it faster, deeper into the protective labyrinth of the volcanic harbor. Jett and Reef, stationed at their posts, squinted into the swirling murk, unable to discern any targets.

"He's slipping away!" Finn yelled, his voice laced with frustration, his hands instinctively reaching for rigging he couldn't see.

Xylar cursed, a guttural sound unfamiliar even to his own ears. His ship's instruments, usually so precise, were being jammed by the overwhelming volcanic dust and the lingering smoke. He could attempt a risky pursuit, but plunging into the uncharted, reef-strewn waters of the inner harbor blind, with his own ship damaged and visibility almost nil, would be suicide. His ship might be advanced, but even it couldn't see through solid rock or avoid unseen shoals.

The sounds of The Black Kraken's retreat faded into the churning smoke. When the air finally began to clear, revealing the stark, volcanic landscape once more, the inner harbor was empty. Neither ship was destroyed, a testament to their immense power and resilience. But in the chaos and blinding smoke of the battle, the Black Kraken had managed to escape, vanishing into the depths of Malakor's fortress-island.

The crew of The Revenge of the Sea Serpent stood on their battered deck, breathing heavily, their faces streaked with soot and sweat. Their ship, though damaged, was still afloat, a silent testament to their triumph against overwhelming odds. But the ultimate prize, Redtooth Malakor, had slipped through their fingers. The rage, momentarily quenched by battle, now burned with renewed intensity, mixed with bitter frustration. The battle might be over, but the hunt was not. They had driven the Kraken to its lair. Now, they had to kill it.

Chapter 29: The Aftermath: A Bruised Victory

The smoke slowly cleared, revealing the battered but defiant Revenge of the Sea Serpent, a silent testament to the brutal duel it had just endured. The deck was a chaos of splintered wood, charred plating, and dislodged equipment. The air still hummed with the phantom echoes of explosions and the acrid scent of sulfur and ozone. Xylar, still at the helm, released a breath he hadn't realized he was holding. Malakor had escaped, a bitter pill to swallow, but they had stood against The Black Kraken and lived.

"Damage report!" Xylar's voice, though strained, cut through the daze. His sharp, calculating mind immediately shifted from combat to assessment.

Finn, his face smudged with soot but his movements still precise, was already barking orders to other crewmen. "Main sail torn, Cap'n! Starboard bow plating compromised, a few more direct hits there and we'd have been swimming! Secondary power conduits rerouted, but we're running at about sixty percent efficiency. Minor fires below deck are out, but the air's thick."

Grog, wiping blood from a gash on his forehead, grunted, "We lost a few good men, Cap'n... caught in the broadsides.

And Pip's got a nasty burn, but he'll live." His voice was heavy with the losses, even amidst their victory. Jett and Reef, though shaken, were already diligently helping with the cleanup, their small hands working to clear debris and secure loose gear.

Xylar nodded grimly, his gaze sweeping over his bruised and weary crew. They were alive, but not unscathed. He knew the limits of his unique technology; even the Revenge, with its self-repairing systems, needed time and resources to fully recover from such a pounding. Pushing on now would be reckless, a foolish move that would put them all in needless peril.

"Alright," Xylar declared, his voice firm, "we've pushed the Kraken from its lair. We've shown Malakor he faces a force unlike any other. But we're damaged, and so is he. We'll regroup. Lyra, plot a course for the nearest neutral port. One with good facilities for repairs and resupply. We'll lick our wounds, bury our dead, and then we finish this."

As Xylar turned from the helm, planning the next phase of their relentless hunt, a sharp gasp cut through the organized chaos of the damage assessment.

"Cap'n! You're hurt!" Lyra exclaimed, rushing towards him.

Xylar instinctively tried to hide it, a subtle shift in his stance, but it was too late. A jagged shard of splintered wood, driven by a powerful impact, had pierced his side, tearing through his jacket and shirt. The wound wasn't bleeding profusely, but it was deep, and a dark, viscous fluid, unlike anything Lyra had ever seen, was seeping from it. It was thick, almost oily, and pulsed with a faint, iridescent glow.

"It's just… a scratch," Xylar began, trying to dismiss her. His human disguise, usually so robust, had been compromised.

"A scratch?!" Lyra retorted, her voice edged with alarm as she carefully peeled back the torn fabric. Her eyes widened, not just at the depth of the wound, but at the unnerving sight beneath. Where human flesh should have been, there was an intricate, pulsing network of glowing, vein-like tendrils, interwoven with shimmering, almost crystalline tissue. The strange fluid continued to well from the wound, shimmering in the dim light. "What in the blazes…?"

Chapter 30: The Truth Will Set You Free

Xylar knew the jig was up. The shock on Lyra's face, the growing murmurs of the curious crew who had gathered around them, and the undeniable evidence laid bare. He sighed, a human gesture he had picked up to convey resignation. "Gather the crew," he said, his voice quiet but commanding. "All hands. I have something to tell you."

The remaining crew – Grog, Rory, Finn, Stoke, Pip, Jett, Reef, and the rest – assembled on the battered main deck. The grim reality of the battle's toll mingled with a bewildered curiosity about their captain's wound. Xylar stood before them, his injured side throbbing, the strange wound now visible to all, shimmering faintly in the morning light.

He took a deep breath, looking at each of their faces. "My name," he began, his voice surprisingly steady, "is not truly Xylar. Not in the way you understand it. I am… not from here. Not from your world, or your kind."

Then, he began to explain. He spoke of his true form, a being of energy and light. He told them of Project Terra, a simple observation mission. He described the hurricane, the crash, the desperate, dying act of his ship's AI to synthesize a human body, to allow him to "blend." He spoke of the Stardust Wanderer, and how its shattered remnants, combined with the lost plank of The Sea Serpent, had forged the very vessel they stood upon, endowing it with its impossible speed and resilience. He revealed the nature of its hidden hum, its silent cannons, its improbable repairs. He left out little, from his initial confusion with human customs to his desperate, solitary work constructing their ship.

The reaction was immediate and visceral.

Some screamed, recoiling in horror, their eyes wide with disbelief and primal fear. The concept of an alien being, a creature from beyond their world, was too much to bear. Jett instinctively grabbed Reef's hand, both their faces pale with a mixture of terror and wide-eyed confusion.

Some threw up, their stomachs churning with a mixture of fear and profound disorientation. The world they knew, their very understanding of reality, had been irrevocably shattered.

Some didn't comprehend, their minds simply refusing to process the fantastic, impossible truth. They stared blankly, their eyes glazed over, as if Xylar were speaking in a forgotten tongue.

Grog stumbled backward, clutching his chest, his booming voice reduced to a strangled gasp. Pip, young and imaginative, looked terrified, then utterly fascinated, his eyes fixed on the strange wound. Rory, who had seen enough horrors, merely blinked, his face pale, slowly processing the unbelievable words.

Lyra and Finn, however, merely exchanged a look. They had always been the suspicious ones, the perceptive observers who knew something was off about their quiet, uncanny captain. The way he spoke, his impossible knowledge, the ship itself – they had always sensed a deeper mystery, a hidden truth. Now, it was laid bare, and while the shock was profound, there was also a strange sense of vindication, of understanding.

"I knew it!" Lyra finally burst out, a half-hysterical laugh escaping her lips. "I knew there was something more than just clever engineering! You're… you're a space man!" She looked at him with a mixture of awe and exasperation.

Finn, ever quiet, simply nodded slowly. "Explains a lot," he murmured, his gaze still steady.

Xylar waited, letting the revelation sink in, allowing them their reactions. When the initial shock began to subside, he spoke again, his voice quiet but resolute. "This is who I am. This ship… it is a part of me, born of my world, but forged with the spirit of yours. I did not ask for this war. It found me. Malakor… he took everything from me. My true mission, my home away from home on the Sea Serpent." He gestured to the battered deck, to the faces of the crew. "You are my family now. This hunt… it is all that matters to me."

He looked at them, his gaze unwavering, vulnerable yet determined. "I understand if you wish to leave. If this… this changes everything for you. But I must know. After all you have seen, all I have revealed… who among you still wishes to fight? Who will still stand with me against Redtooth Malakor?"

The silence stretched, thick with tension and the weight of their choices. Then, slowly, almost imperceptibly, Grog stepped forward. His expression, initially one of bewildered terror, solidified into grim resolve. "Alien or not," he rumbled, his voice regaining some of its thunder, "you took down eight of his ships, and you bruised his Kraken. You're the best bloody captain I've ever sailed under, 'space man' or not! I'm with you, Xylar. To the depths!"

Rory, his eyes still wide, managed a weak grin. "After what I've seen Malakor do, I don't care if you're a kraken yourself, Cap'n. You're our only chance. I'm in!"

Pip, the young powder monkey, his initial fear replaced by wide-eyed wonder, practically bounced. "You built this ship?! You're amazing! I'll fight! I'll fight Malakor till his teeth are clean!"

Jett and Reef, seeing the resolve of their older shipmates, looked at each other, then, still holding hands, stepped forward together. "We're in too, Cap'n!" Jett declared, his voice surprisingly firm. "We'll fight!" Reef nodded vigorously beside him.

One by one, the others voiced their commitment. Stoke gave a curt, almost imperceptible nod, signaling his unwavering loyalty. And finally, Lyra, a mischievous glint back in her eyes, stepped forward. "Well, this certainly makes for a better story than just a regular pirate captain, doesn't it?" she said, offering a wry smile. "And a space man who wants revenge on Malakor? That's a legend I want to be part of. I'm not going anywhere, Cap'n."

Xylar looked at them, his true family, his motley crew of humans. A strange, unfamiliar warmth spread through his chest – a sensation he now recognized as profound relief and a deep, abiding loyalty. They didn't care. They still wanted to be his crew. The repairs would be made, the fallen mourned, and the hunt would continue. This time, with an even greater understanding between captain and crew.

Chapter 31: The Birth of the Space Serpent

The days that followed the brutal clash with The Black Kraken were a whirlwind of activity, a race against time and the chilling memory of their narrow escape. The Revenge of the Sea Serpent, though miraculously still afloat, bore the grievous scars of the epic duel. Splintered wood and twisted plating littered the deck, grim reminders of the furious exchange. The ship's powerful hum, usually a steady thrum, was uneven, a testament to compromised conduits and strained systems below. Xylar, now openly revealing the strange, iridescent glow of his healing wound to his crew, directed the repairs with a focused intensity that seemed to defy exhaustion.

Their destination was a neutral, bustling port where anonymity could be found amidst the cacophony of commerce and countless ships. As they sailed, the crew worked tirelessly, a newly forged unit under their extraordinary captain. The initial shock of Xylar's revelation had, in the crucible of shared danger and his vulnerable honesty, solidified their bond. Now, they were a team driven by a common, impossible purpose.

Grog, with his booming voice and surprising dexterity for a man of his size, oversaw the hauling of replacement timbers and the patching of sailcloth, his commands resounding across the deck. Finn, ever the quiet craftsman, meticulously re-rigged lines and mended torn canvas, his deep understanding of the ship's traditional elements proving invaluable even on this unique vessel. Lyra, with her cunning charm and network of contacts, vanished into the labyrinthine alleys of the port, emerging with vital supplies – rare components Xylar needed for his advanced tech, fresh water, provisions, and, of course, ample stores of rum. Even Pip, his burn healing, found purpose in running messages and fetching tools, his youthful energy tireless. Jett and Reef, though still slightly wide-eyed about their captain's true nature, tirelessly carried smaller bundles of rope and canvas, proving their worth in every task. The repairs were a complex dance between human ingenuity and the ship's unique precision, Xylar guiding them through the intricacies of the Revenge's unusual construction, the crew now understanding the strange materials that hummed beneath their hands.

During a particularly arduous session of patching the starboard hull, the sheer effort giving way to a rare moment of exhausted camaraderie, Grog wiped sweat from his brow and grunted, "This ship, Cap'n... it ain't just the Revenge of the Sea Serpent anymore, is it? Not with all this... magic you got runnin' through her veins." He gestured vaguely at a pulsating panel Xylar was working on, the glow from Xylar's own healing side echoing its strange light.

Rory, perched nearby, helping to secure a new plank with surprising care, chimed in, "Aye! And after what you told us, Xylar... where do you come from? It's more than just sea and vengeance, ain't it?"

A thoughtful silence fell over the small group gathered around the hull. The revelation of Xylar's true nature had been a profound shock, certainly, but in the crucible of battle and shared purpose, it had solidified their bond, not broken it. They had faced the impossible alongside him, and the impossible had proven to be their greatest strength. They were rebuilding more than a ship; they were forging a new identity for themselves and their vessel.

Then, Lyra, always quick with a word and a mischievous glint in her eyes, straightened up from securing a lashed-down crate of fresh fruit. "Well, if we're going to sail with a 'space man' and a ship that's half star-stuff, half old Sea Serpent plank," she said, tapping the very plank Xylar had integrated into the hull, the wood a tangible link to their past, "then perhaps she needs a name that truly honors all of it. A name that speaks to where we've been, and where we're going."

She looked at Xylar, then at the familiar plank that bore Elara's ship's faded name. "We honor the Sea Serpent," she began, her voice gaining strength, "and we honor where our captain comes from. What about... The Space Serpent?"

The words hung in the air, then a low murmur rippled through the small group, quickly growing into excited chatter.

"The Space Serpent," Finn repeated softly, a rare smile touching his lips, as if testing the sound on his tongue. "It fits. Like she's risen from the stars and the depths, all at once."

Grog let out a booming laugh that cut through the port's distant din. "Aye! Gives the bloody Kraken something else to chew on! 'Beware the Space Serpent!' I like the sound of that!" He clapped Xylar on the shoulder, a gesture of deep, newfound camaraderie.

Pip, his face alight with renewed wonder, punched the air. "The Space Serpent! That's brilliant!" Jett and Reef, mimicking Pip, chorused the name, their initial trepidation replaced by unbridled enthusiasm.

Xylar looked at them, his crew, his family. The name was perfect. It wasn't just a new nickname; it was a testament to their shared journey, a fusion of their past and their extraordinary present. It honored the memory of the Sea Serpent and the people lost, acknowledged his unique origins, and perfectly encapsulated the unique, formidable vessel they now commanded. The repairs continued with renewed vigor, the name The Space Serpent already echoing in their newfound unity, shouted by crewmen throughout the ship. The ship was not just being replenished; it was being reborn, a symbol of defiance and a promise of retribution, ready to face the deepest parts of Malakor's lair.

Chapter 32: Rebirth and Renewed Resolve

Reborn and bearing its new name, The Space Serpent cut through the waves, a sleek, dark phantom of vengeance. The crew, now bound by shared secrets and an unbreakable resolve, had transformed their vessel from a bruised warrior into something more majestic than ever before. Every splintered plank had been meticulously replaced, every torn sail expertly mended, and the powerful hum beneath its deck now throbbed with a steady, confident rhythm that vibrated through the very timbers. The repairs, a testament to both Xylar's advanced knowledge of materials and engineering and the crew's tireless, unified efforts, had truly transformed the ship. Its hull, a seamless fusion of dark, polished hardwood and exotic, unidentifiable metals, gleamed under the tropical sun, subtly pulsing with an inner light that hinted at its otherworldly origins. It was a vessel reborn, not just repaired, but fundamentally renewed, a potent symbol of their unyielding defiance.

The next few days at sea were filled with a profound sense of hope and a vibrant, palpable family vibe that permeated every corner of the ship. The grim silence and taut apprehension that had settled after the brutal, inconclusive battle with Malakor's goons had lifted, replaced by the easy camaraderie of shared purpose and a deepening, almost telepathic bond forged in the fires of revelation and shared vulnerability.

Even Xylar found himself relaxing into this newfound dynamic, a genuine smile gracing his lips more often than his human disguise had previously allowed. He observed his crew with a new lens, no longer just as a scientist meticulously gathering data on fascinating specimens, but as a captain truly connected to his people, his kin. He found himself laughing aloud at Grog's booming tales of impossible tavern brawls and Lyra's quick-witted retorts that could leave a man speechless, or at Finn's dry, unexpected wit. Finn, ever the quiet one, would offer a rare, insightful comment that often cut directly to the heart of the matter, and Rory, though still haunted by the ghosts of his past, found solace in the easy rhythm of ship life and Grog's unwavering, protective friendship. Jett and Reef, no longer just busy, scurrying powder monkeys, listened intently, their faces rapt with wonder at the exploits of their seasoned shipmates, sometimes even interjecting with earnest, small tales of their own childhood adventures. They shared meals under the vast, star-dusted sky, each taking turns to recount tales of their past – the good, the bad, and the utterly ridiculous. In these shared vulnerabilities, their bond solidified, making the ship feel less like a mere vessel of vengeance and more like a true, floating home, a sanctuary in a dangerous world.

Amidst this joyous, almost idyllic time, however, the underlying purpose never wavered. Each laugh, each shared story, was tempered by the acute knowledge of the monumental task ahead. They were not merely sailing; they were preparing to finally, definitively, kill the Kraken. The ship's unique cannons were polished to a mirror sheen, their exotic energy conduits checked and rechecked for any lingering imperfections. Boarding axes were sharpened to a wicked edge that glinted menacingly in the sun, and new strategies for engaging Malakor's formidable flagship were discussed, refined, and practiced in mock drills. There was a quiet intensity beneath the laughter, a coiled readiness, a simmering anticipation for the inevitable, final confrontation. Every swing of a cutlass during practice, every shouted command, every adjustment to the sails, was a step closer to their ultimate vengeance.

The sun beat down, turning the sapphire sea into a shimmering expanse of endless blue. Xylar was on the main deck, sharing a rare moment of genuine levity with Lyra and Finn, discussing the finer points of a particularly outlandish story Grog had told the night before about wrestling a giant squid. Jett and Reef were nearby, practicing knot-tying on a spare coil of rope, their giggles occasionally blending with the adults' subdued laughter. The gentle sounds of the waves lapping against the hull filled the air.

Suddenly, a high-pitched, excited cry, sharp enough to cut through the serene atmosphere, sliced through the sounds of the ship.

"SHIP AHOY!"

The voice was Pip's, clear and piercing, ringing out from the crow's nest, instantly silencing all other sounds. Every head on deck snapped upward as if on a string, every heart skipped a beat, then began to pound with a frantic rhythm. Pip was pointing with an almost frantic energy, his small arm a rigid line against the vast sky, his entire body trembling with the enormity of his discovery.

"It's… It's the Kraken!" he shrieked, his voice cracking with a mixture of raw terror and undeniable triumph. "We found it at last!"

A profound, breathless hush fell over The Space Serpent. The laughter died instantly, the vibrant camaraderie replaced by a sudden, electric tension that seemed to crackle in the air. There, on the distant horizon, a smudge of impossible black against the distant blue, was the unmistakable, terrifying silhouette of The Black Kraken. Larger than life, more ominous than memory. The hunt, for all its unexpected twists and turns, its profound losses and unexpected bonds, had finally, undeniably, come to its ultimate, terrifying conclusion.

The time for talking, for preparation, for camaraderie, was over. The time for the final reckoning had arrived.

Chapter 33: The Chase Through the Ring of Fire

The call of "Kraken!" from Pip in the crow's nest ignited an immediate, primal shift on The Space Serpent. The vibrant camaraderie of moments before snapped into sharp, focused intensity. Laughter died on lips, replaced by grim lines of determination. Xylar, without a moment's hesitation, spun the helm. "Full speed ahead, Finn! Lyra, keep an eye on their heading – they won't outrun us this time!"

The Space Serpent surged forward, its powerful engines roaring to life with a deep, resonant thrum that vibrated through the very deck. The ship, sleek and dark, seemed to leap across the waves, leaving a frothing white wake in its furious pursuit. The gap between them and the Black Kraken, still a dark smudge on the horizon, began to shrink, slowly but surely. Jett and Reef, clinging to a rail on the main deck, their faces a mixture of apprehension and excitement, watched the enemy ship grow larger, the wind whipping their hair.

Malakor, it seemed, had no intention of a straightforward fight in the open sea. As the Space Serpent gained on him, the Kraken suddenly veered sharply, leading them towards a menacing silhouette that had begun to emerge from the morning haze. It was a small ring of mountainous islands, a scattered chain of jagged, volcanic peaks thrusting dramatically from the sea, their slopes dark and forbidding. Jagged spires of rock clawed at the sky, and ominous shadows stretched across the water. It was a natural labyrinth, a dangerous maze of narrow channels, hidden reefs, and sheer rock faces.

"He's leading us into the Devil's Teeth!" Grog roared, his excitement tinged with a healthy dose of apprehension as he peered through his spyglass. "Smart, that devil! Knows these waters like his own rotten soul! Plenty of places to hide, or to run us aground!"

The chase transformed into an epic, high-stakes game of cat and mouse amidst the treacherous terrain. The Black Kraken, despite its immense size, navigated the narrow passages with chilling expertise, using the towering mountains as natural barriers and blockers. It would vanish behind a jagged peak, its dark hull momentarily swallowed by shadow, only to reappear moments later, seemingly in a different spot, forcing Xylar to make split-second navigational decisions. The air filled with the shriek of wind, the slap of waves, and the distant, taunting creak of the Kraken's timbers.

The Space Serpent, with Xylar at the helm and Finn expertly adjusting the sails, pursued with relentless precision. Its incredible agility allowed it to execute turns and maneuvers that would have grounded any other vessel. They snaked through narrow gaps barely wider than their hull, skirted sheer cliffs where spray exploded against rock, and barely avoided hidden shoals that would have torn their belly open. A few opportunistic shots were fired from both sides during this desperate evasive battle, the air punctuated by the crack of conventional cannons and the hum of energy blasts. Cannonballs screamed past, showering the decks with stinging spray and rock dust where they impacted the surrounding islands. Energy bolts from the Space Serpent scorched the volcanic mountainsides, sending plumes of ash and debris raining down onto the water. There were many close calls, the wind whipping fiercely through their rigging as they narrowly avoided collisions, the very rock faces seeming to scrape past their painted hull. Miraculously, no one got a direct hit. Both captains were too focused on maneuvering, too intent on using the environment to their advantage, each waiting for the other to make a fatal mistake.

"He's trying to shake us off!" Lyra yelled, her voice strained as she tracked the Kraken's disappear behind another large island, her hand hovering over the ship's communication panel. "He knows we can't risk a full broadside in these tight channels! We'll tear ourselves apart!" The frustration was palpable, a growing knot in the stomach of every crewman.

Chapter 34: The Trap is Sprung: Mountains as Weapons

The chase continued, a furious, dizzying dance of ships and rock. Xylar, his brow furrowed in deep concentration, was pushing The Space Serpent to its absolute limits, matching Malakor's every cunning turn. The raw power of their engines was a constant growl beneath them, but the realization gnawed at him: in this environment, their superior firepower was largely nullified. They couldn't get a clear shot without risking grounding themselves or hitting the surrounding peaks, and Malakor was a master of evasion in this labyrinth.

Just as Xylar felt a surge of cold frustration, a new voice cut through the tense quiet on the bridge, it was Stoke, the quiet, grizzled bosun, his eyes narrowed to slits, staring intently at the constantly shifting, treacherous landscape.

"Cap'n," he rumbled, his voice rough but clear, cutting through the wind, "We ain't gonna hit him like this. Not clean, anyway. Not without risking our own neck. But… we don't have to hit him."

Xylar turned, intrigued, a flicker of hope in his eyes. "Go on, Stoke. What do you see?"

"These rocks," Stoke continued, gesturing to the towering peaks that formed their impromptu arena, their dark surfaces scarred by ancient flows. "Volcanic. Loose. And those guns of yours, Cap'n, they hit harder than any twenty cannons I've ever seen." He paused, his gaze meeting Xylar's, then the grim, daring realization dawned on Xylar. "Instead of shooting at the Kraken, Cap'n... shoot the mountains."

A dangerous, exhilarating grin spread across Xylar's face, a sudden, almost wild spark in his eyes. It was utterly reckless, perfectly human in its audacity, and brilliantly effective. "A stroke of genius, Stoke!" he boomed, turning to his crew. "Finn, Lyra, get ready for extreme evasive action! Grog, prepare the crew for heavy tremors – secure anything that isn't bolted down! Stoke, get your gunners ready! Jett, Reef, stay clear of the main deck and hold onto something solid! Target the highest, most unstable-looking rock formations directly above the Kraken's path! We're not just blocking his escape, we're bringing the mountain down on him!"

The plan was relayed through the speaking tubes. A cheer, wild and fierce, erupted from the crew. This was a pirate's solution, a brutal, poetic justice, using the very environment against their foe. The atmosphere on deck transformed from tense pursuit to grim anticipation, a hungry readiness for the unique destruction they were about to unleash.

As the Black Kraken emerged from behind a massive, sheer cliff face, its crew, perhaps thinking they had finally gained some distance, the Space Serpent veered sharply, not towards the enemy ship, but directly towards the mountain peak towering above it. The target was clear, ominous, and impossible to miss.

"FIRE!" Xylar roared, his voice cutting through the rising wind, a command that reverberated through the very core of the Space Serpent.

The Space Serpent's energy cannons unleashed a synchronized, devastating barrage. But this time, their targets were not the Kraken's hull, but the precariously balanced, millennia-old rock formations high above its path. The concentrated energy blasts struck the volcanic rock with unimaginable force, searing into its dark surface. The air filled with a thunderous, ear-splitting roar, a cacophony of sound that echoed and rebounded off the surrounding islands, shaking the very air. The mountain groaned, then shuddered, protesting the sudden, immense assault, deep cracks spiderwebbing across its ancient face.

Then, with a terrifying, groaning rumble that vibrated through the very water beneath their hull, an enormous section of the peak began to give way. Boulders the size of ships, followed by cascades of smaller rocks and dust, began to rain down with terrifying speed and destructive force. A torrent of earth and stone, an avalanche of vengeance, thundered towards the hapless Kraken.

Malakor, on the deck of The Black Kraken, watched in horrified disbelief, his face draining of all color. He screamed orders, his voice raw and desperate, trying to turn his ship, to move clear, but it was too late. The deluge was upon them. The first massive chunk of rock slammed into The Black Kraken's mainmast, tearing it from its base with a sickening crack that was drowned out by the thunder of the falling mountain. Another boulder crashed through the deck, then another, and another, smashing through timber and iron alike, ripping through the very heart of the ship.

The Kraken, battered and overwhelmed, bucked violently, its remaining sails now shredded by falling debris. Its once menacing hull groaned under the immense weight, its masts splintered into kindling, its decks ravaged beyond recognition. It sat, a broken, helpless giant, pinned against the towering rock wall, waiting for the inevitable, final destruction. The sea churned around it, roiling with displaced water and falling debris, as if the ocean itself recoiled from the devastation. Malakor's ship, the symbol of his terror, was now reduced to a crippled, ignominious ruin, its reign of fear coming to a thunderous, crushing end.

Chapter 35: Approaching the Silent Giant

The thunderous roar of the collapsing mountain slowly faded, replaced by the ominous creak of straining timbers and the hungry crackle of fire consuming wood. The Black Kraken, once the undisputed terror of the seas, now sat a broken, pathetic ruin, crushed beneath immense boulders, its masts snapped like kindling, its decks ripped open to the sky. The silence that followed the cacophony of destruction was profound, almost unsettling, a chilling testament to the sheer power unleashed.

The Space Serpent, a dark, unblemished predator against the morning sky, began its slow, cautious approach. Every eye on board was fixed on the crippled behemoth, their faces a mix of grim satisfaction and an unspoken unease. The crew, hardened by battle and bound by a shared quest for vengeance, gripped their weapons, their adrenaline still pumping, ready for any last, desperate act of defiance. Jett and Reef stood at the rails, their earlier excitement at the mountain's fall replaced by a wide-eyed awe at the sheer scale of the devastation, their small hands gripping the cold metal. Yet, as they drew closer, a strange quiet settled over them. The expected shouts of defiance, the desperate pleas for quarter, the last, furious burst of cannon fire — none of it came. All that could be heard was the mournful sound of waves crashing against the wounded hull and the relentless, hungry roar of the flames steadily consuming the Kraken's interior, casting flickering, demonic shadows.

"Cap'n," Grog rumbled, his voice low, breaking the heavy silence that hung in the air like a shroud. "Somethin' ain't right. Too quiet."

Xylar, his sharp vision already piercing the smoke and debris, felt it too – a chilling absence that prickled at his senses. He could discern no movement, no frantic scurrying, no sign of life beyond the flickering shadows cast by the fires and the slow, inevitable creep of destruction. He brought The Space Serpent alongside the Kraken's crippled port side, maneuvering with exquisite precision until their hulls almost touched, a silent behemoth next to a dying one.

"Boarding party, prepare!" Xylar commanded, his voice tight with a suppressed tension that belied his outward calm. "Lyra, Finn, Stoke, Grog, Rory – with me. Pip, Jett, Reef, you stay on the Space Serpent with the main crew. Stand ready with the reserve firepots and keep your eyes peeled. Be ready for anything." The two young boys, though eager to join, nodded, understanding the gravity of their watch.

As the boarding plank slammed against the Kraken's mangled deck, a wave of acrid smoke, thick with the scent of burning wood and ozone, billowed out, forcing them to shield their faces. The deck was a scene of utter devastation, a testament to the mountain's wrath. It was strewn with colossal chunks of rock, splintered wood, torn rigging, and the grim evidence of the battle. They moved cautiously, weapons raised, their boots crunching on debris and shattered glass.

"No one," Lyra murmured, her eyes darting through the wreckage, a note of disbelief echoing in the desolate silence. "There's no one here. Not a soul to fight."

Indeed, the Kraken was eerily empty. No desperate defenders, no last stand, just the stillness of death and ruin. Their search revealed only a few gruesome sights: the dead bodies of Malakor's crew, grotesquely crushed beneath the massive rocks that had rained down from the mountain, their forms entombed in the very destruction they had wrought. But the vast majority of the crew, and more importantly, Malakor himself, were conspicuously absent.

A cold realization dawned on Xylar, sharp and bitter. Malakor was no fool. He had recognized the impossible threat of The Space Serpent, witnessed the inexplicable destruction of his own ships, and understood the tactical brilliance of bringing down an entire mountain. He had used the very chaos of the attack – the blinding smoke, the deafening roar of the falling rock, the widespread destruction –perfect cover for his escape.

Xylar stepped to the shattered rail, his gaze sweeping over the scene of destruction, then across the water to the towering, jagged island from which the rocks had fallen. It was heavily forested in parts, its slopes rising sharply, offering countless hiding places within its natural labyrinth. And nearby, where the massive chunks of mountain had detached, the terrain was a treacherous mix of newly fallen debris and jagged, untouched rock, providing perfect cover for a desperate retreat.

"He's gone," Xylar stated, his voice flat, the hard-won victory turning to ash in his mouth. "He abandoned ship in the chaos." He slammed a fist against the mangled rail, the frustration a bitter sting that he allowed himself to show for a brief moment. "He's hidden himself somewhere on the island. Among those mountains, in the forests... or perhaps even within the debris of the fallen peak."

The great duel was over, the Kraken broken and burning, but the head of the beast, Redtooth Malakor, had once again slipped through their grasp. The hunt, it seemed, was far from over. It had merely moved to dry land. The final reckoning awaited them on solid ground, an uncharted territory for the Space Serpent's crew.

Chapter 36: A New Kind of Hunt

The return to The Space Serpent was somber. The triumphant adrenaline of breaking The Black Kraken had evaporated, replaced by a gnawing frustration. Malakor, the architect of their suffering, had once again slipped through their grasp, leaving behind only the smoldering carcass of his ship. The crew gathered on the main deck, the ship's hum a low thrum beneath their feet, their eyes fixed on the distant, jagged peaks of the island where Malakor had vanished.

Xylar, typically composed even in the face of the impossible, felt a ripple of profound unease. He could command his great warship, predict complex atmospheric shifts, and even unravel the mysteries of advanced technology, but close-quarters combat, the visceral, brutal clash of steel and flesh on uneven ground, was a different matter entirely. He was a scientist, not a warrior. As his mind replayed the image of Malakor's predatory grin, and the horrors he'd witnessed that fateful day he first met the Kraken — the ease with which Malakor had cut down Elara's crew, the sickening thud of bodies, the glint of the pirate captain's cruel blade — a cold knot formed in his stomach. He was not a swordsman. He was no match for Malakor in a direct, hand-to-hand fight.

He was snapped back to reality by the subtle shift in the air, the collective gaze of his crew. They could tell he was nervous, a flicker of vulnerability in his usually unreadable demeanor. Even Jett and Reef, clinging to each other slightly, watched him with concerned, questioning eyes.

"Cap'n?" Lyra's voice was soft, laced with concern, breaking the tense silence. "You alright? You look like you've seen a ghost."

Xylar sighed, a long, weary exhalation that was surprisingly human. He looked at them, his newfound family, who had accepted his true nature and fought so fiercely by his side. He owed them honesty. "I am… apprehensive," he admitted, his voice a low rumble. "We broke his ship, yes. But he is still out there, on that island. And this next part of the hunt… it will be on land. It will be up close." He paused, meeting each of their eyes, his gaze steady despite his confession. "I can command this vessel. I can bring down mountains with it. But I am no swordsman. I remember that day when he boarded the Sea Serpent. I remember the ease with which he… extinguished them. I am not skilled in such combat." His words hung in the air, a raw confession of his limitations, stripping away the aura of invincibility they might have perceived.

A beat of silence followed, then Grog stepped forward, a sympathetic grunt escaping him. "Aye, Cap'n. That's a memory no man should carry alone. And it's true, you're a mind, not just a fist." He clapped Xylar on the shoulder, a gesture of rough comfort and profound acceptance. "But you ain't alone now. And you don't gotta be a fancy blade-dancer. That's what we're for." He tapped the hilt of his own heavy cutlass.

Finn, ever practical, nodded, his eyes fixed on Xylar's. "You got us where we needed to be, Cap'n. You gave us the tool, the best damn ship on these seas. Now we use our tools." He unbuckled his cutlass, its worn hilt testifying to years of use, and drew it, the blade glinting in the fading light. "I've faced enough boarding parties and skirmishes on land to know a trick or two. And Malakor's brutes, they hit hard, but they ain't always clever."

Rory, his eyes still holding a shadow of pain from his past, gripped his own sword, the scarred knuckles white. "I spent years as a privateer before Malakor took my ship. I know how to fight dirty. And when you're fighting a monster like him, there's no such thing as 'fair' anyway."

Lyra, ever the strategist, flashed a quick, reassuring smile, her hand briefly resting on Xylar's arm. "Think of us as your personal bodyguard, Cap'n. Your… specialized combat unit. You focus on the strategy, the big picture. We'll make sure no one gets close enough to tickle your... alien bits." Her humor, though dark, drew a few strained chuckles from the crew, easing the tension with familiar camaraderie.

And then, as the sun dipped below the horizon, painting the sky in fiery oranges and purples, they began. One by one, crewmen stepped forward. Finn demonstrated a quick parry and riposte, emphasizing balance and footwork, his movements fluid and precise. Grog, despite his bulk, showed how to use sheer force to overwhelm an opponent's guard, demonstrating powerful, bone-jarring swings. Rory taught a few brutal, no-nonsense disarming techniques, fast and effective. Even Pip, his burn wrapped, eagerly shared a few sling tricks he'd learned in the crowded alleys of Tortuga, showing how to launch small, stinging rocks with surprising accuracy. Jett and Reef watched with wide-eyed fascination, absorbing every movement, even mimicking some of the simpler stances with their own small sticks.

Xylar, ever the student, absorbed it all with the incredible processing power of his mind. Though unused to such physical disciplines, his consciousness rapidly processed the movements, the angles, the shifts in weight. He practiced with them, holding a borrowed cutlass. His initial awkwardness slowly gave way to a more fluid, if still nascent, proficiency. His blows gained force, his parries became surer, his steps more deliberate. They talked strategy long into the night, breaking down the island's treacherous terrain, imagining Malakor's likely hiding spots. They planned their approach, their formation for the trek, and their escape routes if needed, considering every variable.

As night fully descended, casting the island in ominous shadows, the deck of The Space Serpent became a training ground, a place of shared purpose and growing confidence. The air hummed not just with the ship's engines, but with the quiet resolve of a family preparing for war. For in the morning, the final hunt would truly begin. It was time to slay the beast. The reckoning was at hand.

Chapter 37: The Land Assault Plan

As dawn approached, painting the eastern sky in muted greys, Xylar gathered his key crew members on the main deck. The air was cool and crisp, carrying the scent of salt and distant earth, a stark departure from the familiar tang of the open ocean. This was a new battlefield, a new kind of hunt, and Xylar, despite his alien capabilities, knew this was where human grit and experience would truly shine. He laid out the final, meticulous details of their land assault, his voice low but resonant with authority.

"Our primary objective is Malakor," Xylar stated, his gaze sweeping across Finn, Rory, Grog, Stoke, and Lyra. "Alive or dead. Our secondary objective is to neutralize any remaining loyalists and locate his rumored hidden vault or stronghold within this island. He wouldn't have abandoned his ship without a bolt-hole, a place to regroup his remaining forces and hoard his ill-gotten gains."

He spread a rough map he'd meticulously sketched, using his unique perception to detail elevation changes, water sources, and areas of dense foliage, a map far more precise than any human chart. "We will move as one unit for the initial sweep," Xylar affirmed, his gaze meeting each of the chosen land party. "Splitting up in unknown territory against a cunning foe like Malakor would be folly. Our strength lies in our unity, and our ability to cover each other's weaknesses."

"Finn, your unparalleled tracking skills will lead us, reading every broken twig and displaced stone. Rory, you will guard our rear and watch for ambushes, your instincts honed by years of privateering. Grog and Stoke, your combined strength and experience in close-quarters skirmishes will be vital for any direct confrontation, clearing our path through resistance. And Lyra, your sharp mind for observation and patterns, your ability to quickly analyze our surroundings, will be our eyes and ears, guiding our path through the terrain and spotting what others miss. We will move silently, prioritize stealth, and ensure we always have eyes on each other. My own enhanced senses will help us pinpoint disturbances, hidden trails, or thermal signatures, but your combined human experience and adaptability are our greatest asset on this unfamiliar ground." Xylar paused, allowing his words to sink in, emphasizing the critical role each of them played in this unified front. "We are one blade, and that blade must cut true."

"For general challenges," Xylar continued, his gaze sweeping over them, acknowledging the dangers beyond Malakor's men. "We will be facing unknown numbers in their territory, likely using the dense forest and treacherous rock as their allies. The terrain itself is an enemy, with hidden pitfalls, slippery slopes, and sharp volcanic rock. Each of you will carry extra water, basic rations, and bandages – prepare for a sustained operation. Weapons are to be kept concealed until needed; our element of surprise is paramount. Our advantage is our discipline, our unity, and our unwavering resolve."

He then turned to the younger members of the crew, their faces alight with a mixture of anticipation and quiet solemnity. "Pip, Jett, and Reef," Xylar addressed them directly, "you will remain on The Space Serpent with the reserve crew. Your task is not less, it is vital. You are our lifeline, our eyes from above. Maintain a constant, unblinking watch on the island, particularly the shorelines and any sign of movement from the jungle. If we signal for extraction, or if you spot any unusual vessel approaching, you are to alert Stoke immediately and be ready to deploy the longboat with utmost speed. No heroics on your part unless directed. Your job is to keep this ship safe, to be our secure base, and to be our escape if necessary. Your sharp eyes and quick thinking will be the difference between success and disaster."

Their unique training from the night before, a blend of traditional pirate tactics and Xylar's analytical approach, would be paramount. The land party would proceed cautiously, but with an unwavering, focused determination. The Space Serpent's incredible speed and firepower, though remaining offshore, would be their powerful, silent guardian, used for support or extraction if needed. But the decisive blow, the final confrontation with Malakor, would have to be struck by hand, on the treacherous soil of his own lair.

For in the morning, the final hunt would truly begin. It was time to slay the beast. The reckoning was at hand.

Chapter 38: The Island's Embrace: Peril and Steel

The moment their boots touched the volcanic sand, the nature of the hunt shifted dramatically. The predictable roll of waves and the confined decks of ships gave way to the unpredictable hazards of the land. The island was a primordial wilderness, a maze of sharp, black volcanic rock, dense, almost impenetrable jungle, and treacherous, hidden ravines that yawned like hungry mouths. The air hung thick and humid, heavy with the scent of damp earth, rich vegetation, and a faint, ever-present tang of sulfur.

Their initial progress was painstakingly slow. Xylar, using his heightened alien senses, became their living compass and warning system. He detected subtle atmospheric shifts, minute vibrations in the earth, and faint magnetic anomalies that suggested hidden dangers or recent passage. "To the left, there's a geothermal vent," he'd warn, guiding them away from steaming cracks in the ground where noxious fumes escaped. "Avoid that patch of vegetation, the soil is unstable beneath." They moved with extreme caution, navigating narrow ledges where a single misstep meant a long, final fall into the crashing waves below. Every rustle of leaves, every distant bird call, was scrutinized.

They faced immediate environmental dangers that reminded them they were far from the familiar sea. A sudden, localized rockslide, triggered by the recent mountain collapse, sent a shower of sharp debris cascading down a slope they were traversing. Grog, with his immense strength, managed to brace a precarious rock formation, holding it just long enough for Lyra and Rory to scramble past, while Finn expertly guided Xylar out of the direct path of the falling stones. Moments later, they almost stumbled into a hidden fissure, a deep, smoking chasm veiled by thick foliage, Xylar's alien senses warning them just in time, allowing Stoke to swiftly mark the danger for the others.

It was in a particularly dense, shadowed part of the forest, where the air was thick and humid, and the light struggled to penetrate the canopy, that the first ambush came. A barely audible rustle in the undergrowth, a glint of steel, and then three figures burst from the shadows – Malakor's men. They were not common thugs, but hardened veterans, their faces grim, their eyes cold with fanatic loyalty. These were Redtooth's most trusted, sent to slow, maim, and kill the intruders.

The first pirate, a burly brute wielding a heavy broadsword, lunged at Xylar. Xylar, recalling Finn's rapid lessons, managed a clumsy parry, deflecting the blow with a jarring clang that sent vibrations up his arm. But the pirate was fast, pressing the attack relentlessly. Before Xylar could fully recover, Grog moved like a whirlwind of muscle, his axe swinging in a wide, powerful arc that forced the pirate to leap back. Grog then engaged the brute in a brutal, clashing exchange of heavy blows, each strike capable of shattering bone.

Lyra, meanwhile, danced with a swift, agile opponent, her pistols spitting fire, forcing him to keep his distance before she closed with her cutlass, her movements fluid and deadly, a blur of steel and precision. Finn, a master of the blade, engaged another pirate in a duel of calculated precision, his cutlass a blur of feints and parries, seeking the opening with lethal grace. Stoke, musket at the ready, provided covering fire and watched their flanks, his keen eyes scanning for more threats.

These were no ordinary skirmishes. These were desperate, brutal clashes for survival on uneven ground. The clang of steel echoed through the dense forest, mingling with the shouts and grunts of combatants. Xylar, watching Grog's furious exchange, marveled at the sheer, raw power. He saw Lyra's finesse, her ability to outmaneuver and disarm. And Finn... Finn was a whirlwind of practiced steel, every movement efficient, every parry flawless. The unified unit moved with an instinctual coordination that spoke of battles fought side-by-side, even if this specific environment was new.

The first three fell, their bodies crumpling silently into the undergrowth. Then, as they pushed deeper, guided by Xylar's senses and Finn's tracking, they encountered more. A hidden patrol of five, their ambush thwarted by Xylar's early warning, then another group of two attempting to flank them from a narrow defile. Each encounter was a desperate, bloody struggle, a testament to Malakor's pervasive influence and the loyalty of his remaining crew. Xylar, finding his footing with each new blow, managed to land a few solid blocks, even a clumsy but effective disarming blow that sent a pirate's cutlass clattering onto the rocks. He realized that while he lacked the experience, his alien physiology provided an underlying advantage – faster reflexes, slightly greater strength, and an ability to process opponents' movements with surprising clarity, almost a slow-motion perception of their attacks.

In one particularly harrowing exchange, Xylar found himself isolated for a moment, facing two of Malakor's fiercest men simultaneously. He parried a thrust from one, felt the scrape of steel against his side as the other tried to flank him, a sharp pain reminding him of his mortality. He remembered Rory's grunted lesson: fight dirty. He lashed out with a sudden, unexpected kick, catching one pirate off balance, then used the momentum to spin and deliver a desperate, wild swing that sent the other stumbling. Before they could recover, Finn and

Rory arrived, cutting down Xylar's assailants with ruthless efficiency, their movements a lethal dance.

"You're learning, Cap'n," Finn grunted, a flicker of approval in his eyes as he wiped blood from his blade.

They were relentless. They stalked through the dense undergrowth, flushing out Malakor's hidden defenders, their fury mounting with each encounter, each fallen foe a step closer to their ultimate target. The pirates, though skilled and loyal, were dwindling, their numbers less than Xylar had initially imagined, a sign that Malakor had truly abandoned most of his forces.

Finally, after what felt like an eternity of cautious movement and brutal skirmishes, they found the last of Redtooth's personal guard – a group of ten men, heavily armed and entrenched on a rocky outcrop overlooking a narrow pass. This was the final, desperate line of defense before Malakor's ultimate hiding place. The air crackled with anticipation, the final confrontation drawing near.

The ensuing battle was a furious, desperate crescendo. Malakor's men fought with the ferocity of cornered beasts, knowing this was their last stand. The clashing of steel was deafening, a relentless drumbeat of combat echoing across the natural amphitheater. Grog was a force of nature, his axe cleaving through pirate defenses, scattering foes. Lyra moved like a shadow, striking with blinding speed and accuracy. Finn was an artist of the blade, dancing through the chaos, his cutlass a silver blur, every move a death sentence. Rory, fueled by his own ghosts, fought with a savage intensity, his sabre a vengeful extension of his will. Stoke, a rock amidst the storm, kept the pressure on with musket shots and swift, heavy blows from his own cutlass, ensuring no pirate broke ranks.

Xylar, no longer just observing, fought alongside them. He parried, he dodged, he lunged, his movements gaining a fluidity born of desperation, instinct, and newfound skill. He took a few glancing blows, the impact rattling him, but he gave more, his alien strength surprising his opponents. When the last pirate fell, a guttural cry was silenced mid-air. The silence that descended was absolute, broken only by their ragged breaths, the distant sounds of the sea, and the drip of blood onto the volcanic rock. They had overcome the island's embrace, and now, Malakor was within reach.

Chapter 39: The Final Piece of the Puzzle

They stood amidst the fallen, exhausted but victorious. All ten of Malakor's final defenders were defeated, their bodies sprawled across the rocky outcrop, a testament to the brutal, grinding fight. The silence that followed the last, desperate clash was heavy, broken only by their ragged breaths and the distant sounds of the sea. But they needed more than just victory over Malakor's guard. They needed Malakor himself.

One of the pirates, a burly, scarred man with a defiant sneer still plastered on his bloodied face, was miraculously still alive, pinned beneath a fallen rock. His leg was twisted at an unnatural angle, clearly broken, but his eyes still burned with hatred, fixed on Xylar and his crew. He was the last of them, a grim, living sentinel to Malakor's secrets.

Grog stepped forward, his massive axe heavy in his hand, its blade dripping. His face was a mask of grim determination, devoid of any pity. "Alright, you scurvy dog," he growled, bending over the man, his shadow falling over the pirate. "Where is he? Where's Malakor hiding? Speak, or suffer a far worse fate than a broken leg."

The pirate merely spat blood, a defiant red against the dark rock. "Never!" he rasped, his voice raw but unyielding to the end. "Malakor's secret dies with me! You'll never find him!"

Grog raised his axe slightly, the formidable weapon gleaming, a glint of menace in his eyes that promised unimaginable pain. "We can make this very hard for you, friend. Very, very hard. There are ways to loosen tongues, even stubborn ones."

Xylar stepped forward then, his presence commanding attention, his voice calm, yet resonating with an otherworldly chill that made the pirate's eyes widen, a flicker of genuine fear finally replacing the defiance. "Your defiance is admirable," he said, his tone even, "but ultimately futile. We will find him, with or without your help. The island has yielded its other secrets to us. But if you tell us now, your death will be swift and merciful. If you refuse… the pain will be prolonged. I can assure you, I have knowledge of pain far beyond your comprehension. Knowledge of how to prolong life beyond what is bearable, even when the body screams for release." His eyes, usually human in their disguise, seemed to deepen for a moment, revealing something ancient, cold, and truly terrifying that spoke of suffering on a cosmic scale.

The pirate's last vestige of defiance shattered. He stared into Xylar's eyes, seeing not just a man, but an unfathomable depth of cold, calculated cruelty. A shudder ran through his battered frame. He broke.

"Alright! Alright, demon!" he coughed, pain twisting his face into a grotesque grimace. "He's in… the caldera! The other caldera! Not the big one, you fools! A smaller one! Hidden! There's a fissure… a narrow tunnel… in the side of the highest peak, near the steaming vents! It's masked by vines, a secret entrance he found years ago. He keeps his… his most valuable treasures there. And his true stronghold. He'll be waiting for you. He knows you're coming." The pirate fell back, his strength gone, a flicker of profound fear replacing the defiance, his eyes rolling back as he lost consciousness, or perhaps, life itself.

Xylar exchanged a grim look with his crew. The last piece of the puzzle. The final destination, revealed at last. Malakor's ultimate lair. The very heart of his domain on this cursed island.

"Let's move," Xylar commanded, his voice resolute, the training and the weariness momentarily forgotten in the face of the impending climax. "It's time to slay the beast."

Chapter 40: The Path to the Lair

The weary but resolute crew of The Space Serpent moved with a renewed sense of urgency, the pirate's tortured confession still a raw, unsettling echo in their minds. Malakor's ultimate hiding place was no longer a vague whisper, but a defined destination, a grim beacon drawing them deeper into the island's heart. Their boots crunched on loose volcanic rock as they began the arduous ascent of the winding, jagged paths of the highest peak. The air grew progressively thinner, thick and acrid with the constant, biting smell of sulfur from the active vents the pirate had mentioned. The dense, choking jungle of the lower slopes gradually gave way to more sparse, resilient volcanic scrub, clinging desperately to the harsh, unforgiving rock face, twisted and stunted by the fumes.

As they climbed, the landscape became increasingly alien, a testament to the raw, untamed power of the earth. Steam hissed from countless narrow fissures in the ground, rising in ghostly plumes that created an eerie, almost supernatural atmosphere, swirling and momentarily obscuring their path. The ground beneath their boots was hot in places, pulsating with the raw, untamed energy of the mountain. Every twisted shadow seemed to conceal a lurking threat, and every gust of wind carried the phantom whispers of past horrors. They moved as a single, cohesive unit, a well-oiled machine forged in countless battles, their every movement economical and purposeful.

Grog's immense form, a silent bulwark of muscle and will, led the way through tight, treacherous passes, his heavy boots finding purchase where others would stumble. He tested unstable rocks, his broad shoulders easily pushing aside heavy foliage or loose debris. Finn and Rory, their eyes constantly scanning the treacherous terrain above and below, covered the flanks, their cutlasses loose in their hands, ready for an ambush that could come from any shadow. Stoke brought up the rear, his weathered gaze vigilant, ensuring no one lagged behind or became separated. Lyra's sharp eyes missed nothing, scanning for any sign of ambush, her quick mind already calculating angles and potential escape routes, her focus absolute. Xylar, positioned strategically within the formation, felt the familiar, comforting hum of his ship, now a distant, almost spiritual connection, a promise of retreat should the impossible occur, a symbol of the world he was fighting for.

The silence, save for the hiss of steam and the crunch of their boots, was profound, broken only by Xylar's low, precise warnings about unseen dangers. "Loose scree ahead, proceed with caution," he'd murmur, or, "A thermal fluctuation indicates a hidden fissure to your right." Each step was a testament to their trust in him and his reliance on their raw, human resilience.

They bypassed the main, larger caldera, its vast, smoking mouth a grim testament to the island's destructive power, a maw that could swallow ships whole. Its sheer scale was humbling, a reminder of the raw forces at play on this volatile island. Their true target, the pirate had said, was a smaller, hidden one, a secret lair nestled deep within the mountain's very heart. The air grew warmer, the sulfurous scent more intense, burning in their nostrils. The closer they got, the more their anticipation mounted, their muscles tensing, their resolve hardening with every strenuous, uphill step. This was it. The fight of all fights. The final confrontation.

Finally, after what felt like an eternity of relentless climbing, navigating perilous ledges, and enduring the suffocating sulfuric air, they found it. Tucked away on a seemingly impenetrable, sheer cliff face, hidden behind a shifting veil of steaming vents and dense, sulfuric mist that billowed and swirled, was a dark, jagged fissure in the black rock. It was narrow, barely wide enough for one man to squeeze through at a time, and it plunged into the mountain's depths like a jagged scar, a dark maw leading directly to the beast's lair. The air coming from it was thick with the scent of damp earth, stagnant air, and something else... something metallic and old, a faint, undeniable hint of human habitation within the mountain's cold stone heart. A shiver ran through the group, not of fear, but of grim, determined anticipation. The true hunt was about to begin.

Chapter 41: A Captain's Solitary Burden: The Final Farewell

Xylar stopped at the very entrance to the fissure, the acrid steam stinging his eyes, momentarily blurring his vision. He turned, his gaze sweeping over his battered, courageous crew, allowing himself one last, prolonged look at the faces that had become his world. Their faces, streaked with soot, grime, and the dust of battle, bore the undeniable marks of their relentless journey and the fierce skirmishes they had fought. Grog, immense and unyielding, stood like a mountain himself, a silent promise of brute force. Finn, quiet but solid as the very rock they stood upon, his gaze steady and knowing. Lyra, her sharp wit temporarily dimmed by the gravity of the moment, but her eyes burning with an unyielding loyalty. Rory, his haunted eyes now burning with a singular, fierce determination, reflecting the pain of his own lost past. Stoke stood firm, his veteran's gaze unwavering. They had faced overwhelming odds, accepted an impossible truth about their captain, and stood by him, unwavering, defying logic and expectation. They were his family, forged not by blood, but in the crucible of profound loss and shared vengeance, a bond more profound than any data he could have ever collected.

His heart, that fragile, perplexing human organ he now possessed, ached with a terrible protectiveness, a fierce, almost unbearable tenderness. He remembered Elara's last, desperate command, her voice etched into his very being: "Don't… don't let this break you. Live, Xy. Live for us." He had lost one family already to Malakor's boundless cruelty, the Sea Serpent's crew swallowed by the waves and the pirate's monstrous appetite. He could not, would not, risk losing another. This final confrontation, the ultimate reckoning for all the pain Malakor had inflicted, had to be his alone. The monster that had taken his family would face the one it had inadvertently left behind.

"Listen to me," Xylar began, his voice low, a rough whisper against the hiss of the vents, but carrying the undeniable weight of absolute authority, an unyielding command that even their weary bodies instantly obeyed. He looked at each of them, letting his gaze linger for a moment on their faces, imprinting their expressions on his memory. "We have come this far. You have faced impossible odds. You have fought with courage, with loyalty, with a ferocity that would make any captain, human or otherwise, profoundly proud. You accepted me for what I am, for who I am, when you had every reason to turn away. You are the finest crew a man, or… an alien, could ever wish for."

A lump formed in his throat, a strange, unfamiliar sensation, alien to his true form, yet so acutely human. He swallowed hard, struggling against the emotion that threatened to choke him. "I am profoundly grateful for each and every one of you. You are my family now. My only family."

He paused, taking a deep, shuddering breath, the sulfuric air burning in his lungs. "But this last step… this last fight… it is mine alone." His voice hardened then, infused with an unshakeable, cold resolve that bordered on fanaticism, yet stemmed from deepest love. "He targeted me. He took my family. And I will not risk losing another. Not one of you." His gaze swept over them, daring any protest, silencing it before it could even form. "I cannot risk it. I cannot risk losing you. Not after everything we have endured, everything we have built." He gestured towards the dark, gaping fissure, its depths shrouded in shadow and mist. "Malakor will be waiting. He will be expecting a full assault. This is a trap built for many. But he will not be expecting one. One man, fueled by nothing but vengeance."

He drew the cutlass from his belt, its steel gleaming faintly in the pre-dawn gloom, a stark contrast to his own subtly glowing, rapidly healing wound from the earlier skirmish. "You brought me here. You gave me the means to find him. You taught me how to fight, how to stand against beasts. Now, your task is to wait. To be ready. If I do not emerge… if you hear nothing after a reasonable time… then you will return to The Space Serpent. You will take the ship, and you will sail to freedom, to new horizons. And you will tell our story. The story of The Space Serpent, and the crew who dared to challenge the Kraken."

His eyes, in the dim, pre-dawn light, seemed to shimmer with a faint, otherworldly glow, reflecting the profound love and unbearable loss that warred within him. "I have to go alone. I cannot risk losing another family." With that, he turned towards the dark, steaming fissure, his figure resolute, already consumed by a singular, burning purpose. The fate of their revenge, and his own tormented soul, now rested on his shoulders alone, as he stepped into the gaping mouth of Malakor's lair.

Chapter 42: Into the Dragon's Maw

The fissure swallowed Xylar whole, plunging him into a world of oppressive darkness, scalding heat, and an unsettling quiet. The air was thick, heavy with sulfur and the metallic tang of something ancient and unliving, a faint scent of stale blood lingering beneath. As the narrow opening sealed behind him, cutting off the last sliver of daylight, Xylar drew the cutlass from his belt. The cold steel felt solid and reassuring in his hand, a tangible tether to his crew and the world he fought for, preparing him for the unknown depths ahead.

Each step echoed unnaturally, the sound swallowed by the cavernous blackness. He moved by instinct, his enhanced senses guiding him through the suffocating gloom, a stark contrast to the vast, open expanses he was accustomed to. The heat steadily intensified, a constant, oppressive presence that seeped into his bones, making the air feel like a suffocating blanket.

The passage twisted and turned, a natural tunnel carved by relentless geothermal forces, its walls slick with condensation. In places, an eerie, phosphorescent moss glowed faintly, casting shifting, sickly green light on grotesque rock formations. He navigated treacherous, narrow ledges that dropped into unseen depths, the unsettling scent of the earth's raw power growing stronger with every meter. The journey was unsettling, a descent into a primal, hostile environment, a fitting prelude to the beast he hunted.

Finally, after what felt like an eternity, the narrow confines of the fissure began to widen. The oppressive darkness started to recede, replaced by a dim, hellish glow that pulsed with a malevolent warmth. The air, though still thick with sulfur, stirred with faint currents, hinting at a larger, open space beyond. Xylar pushed through the last, tight squeeze, feeling the rough rock scrape his shoulders, and emerged into a vast, cavernous chamber.

This was no ordinary cave. This was a small, but still grand, caldera, a natural amphitheater of death carved from the very heart of the volcano. The very air pulsed with the heat of the earth, making it feel like stepping into a living, breathing furnace. The ceiling, impossibly high, was a jagged, fractured dome of black volcanic rock, occasionally pierced by thin shafts of light filtering from unseen vents above, illuminating swirling currents of steam and dust. The floor was a treacherous expanse of jagged, obsidian-like rocks, sharp and uneven, interspersed with pools of steaming, sulfurous water that shimmered with an eerie, iridescent sheen. Small, intermittent bursts of flame flickered from cracks in the ground, casting dancing, demonic shadows that seemed to writhe with a life of their own. The raw, untamed walls rose steeply, resembling the gaping maw of some ancient, petrified beast, its breath the hot, sulfuric air.

This was the perfect place for a final battle to the death. It was a crucible, a stage where only the strongest, most determined would survive. There was no escape, no retreat, only the inevitable confrontation.

And there, in the very center of this infernal arena, standing on a raised plateau of flat, black rock, was Redtooth Malakor. He was a hulking, formidable figure, his silhouette framed by the flickering flames, looking every bit the monster Xylar remembered. His distinctive, crimson-stained teeth seemed to gleam even in the dim, infernal light. He held a massive, wickedly curved sword, its blade polished to a mirror sheen, reflecting the hellish glow of the caldera. He was a statue of grim anticipation, his posture radiating a chilling confidence, his eyes fixed on the fissure. He was waiting.

Malakor's eyes, cold and reptilian, fixed on Xylar as he emerged from the fissure, cutlass in hand, bathed in the infernal light. A slow, predatory smile spread across Malakor's face, revealing those dreadful teeth. His voice, a guttural rasp, resonated through the cavern, amplified by the caldera's natural acoustics, carrying a chilling blend of contempt and dark amusement.

"Well, well, well," Malakor began, his voice dripping with mock courtesy, "the little 'Star-Man' returns. Or should I say, the little worm I chose to let live?" He slowly drew his sword, the metallic whisper a chilling prelude, a warning. "I wondered if you'd be foolish enough to follow me into my own domain. I admit, you're more tenacious than I gave you credit for. Word travels fast, even to these forgotten corners. Whispers of a ship that falls from the sky, a captain with eyes like cold stars, seeking vengeance for a ghost."

He took a step forward, his eyes burning with a cruel delight, a predator savoring its prey. "They call you the 'Star-Man' on the docks, you know. A creature of impossible power, yet driven by such mundane, human desires. You took my ships. You broke my Kraken. A commendable effort, for a thing not of this world, clinging to a human disguise. But this is where your luck and your little charade end. This is my forge, alien. My private arena. Here, your fancy tricks and glowing cannons mean nothing. Here, it is just steel and will. And I have more of both than you could ever dream of." He raised his sword, its tip glinting menacingly, a dark promise.

"You speak of revenge, of family," Malakor sneered, a dark chuckle escaping him, echoing unnaturally in the vast chamber. "Such quaint, human notions. I've heard the tales of your impossible journey, your single-minded quest for what I took.

And of what you truly are. But I am the storm, little man. I am the predator. And you are merely prey, walking willingly into my jaws." His smile widened, revealing the full horror of his red-stained teeth. "You came looking for a reckoning, didn't you? Good. Because you found it. Welcome to your demise, Xylar. The very earth you stand on will be your grave. And I will be the one to dig it."

Chapter 43: The Dance of Blades: Xylar vs. Malakor

Malakor lunged, his massive sword a blur of dark steel, aiming to cleave Xylar in two. The blow whistled past Xylar's ear, the sheer force of it ruffling his hair. He dodged, a raw instinct honed by newfound purpose, rolling to the side. His cutlass, firm in his grip, felt strangely light in his hand, an extension of his will, a physical manifestation of his crew's unwavering support.

"A feisty little worm, aren't we?" Malakor sneered, his red-stained teeth gleaming in the infernal light of the caldera. He pressed the attack, his movements surprisingly agile for such a large man, each swing powerful enough to shatter bone. He was a master of overwhelming force, seeking to bludgeon Xylar into submission, roaring with primal fury.

The great battle ensued, a deadly dance of blades across the treacherous, jagged landscape of the caldera. The clang of steel against steel echoed through the vast chamber, a deafening symphony of conflict that filled every crevice. Xylar, still far from a master, fought with every ounce of his being, recalling the rapid-fire lessons from his crew: Finn's precision, Grog's raw power, and Rory's brutal pragmatism. He dodged and parried, a flurry of desperate defensive motions, deflecting blow after devastating blow with a growing, desperate efficiency. Malakor was relentless, his attacks a continuous, overwhelming torrent, each strike a testament to years of blood-soaked experience.

They moved across the entire caldera, their battle a furious maelstrom of movement and sound, their figures silhouetted against the flickering volcanic flames. Xylar used the treacherous terrain to his advantage, leaping onto higher, jagged ledges, forcing Malakor to climb and momentarily disrupting his rhythm, gaining a fleeting respite. He scrambled over jagged rocks, the intense heat from the ground scorching his boots through the thin soles, Malakor hot on his heels, his heavy footfalls shaking the ground. He darted through swirling plumes of superheated steam that erupted from hidden vents, using the temporary obscuration as cover, trying to break Malakor's relentless assault. The pirate, however, was equally adept at using the environment, leveraging his brute strength to smash through fragile rock formations, his heavy blows sending chips of obsidian flying like shrapnel. They exchanged back and forth strikes and blocks, their blades connecting often with jarring, metal-on-metal force, but neither combatant managed to land a decisive blow. It was a brutal test of endurance and skill, a battle of the ages unfolding in a hellish arena.

Minutes bled into an eternity. Xylar's arms began to ache, a burning throb in his muscles, his breath coming in ragged gasps that tasted of sulfur and iron. Malakor, though sweating profusely, showed no signs of tiring, his movements still precise and powerful. He was a veteran, a master of the blade, a living instrument of war, and it slowly, painfully, became clear that even with all the frantic training from his crew, Xylar was no match for Redtooth in a sustained, one-on-one sword duel. Malakor was simply faster, stronger, and infinitely more experienced in the brutal art of close combat.

Malakor began to slowly get the upper hand. His attacks grew more confident, more precise, driving Xylar back across the treacherous ground. He found openings Xylar couldn't cover, forcing Xylar to scramble, to barely deflect blows that would have ended the fight instantly. Malakor began to torment Xylar with taunts, his voice a cruel balm that sought to break his spirit, eroding his will piece by painful piece.

"Is that all, little space-thing?" Malakor sneered, his blade forcing Xylar onto a precarious, crumbling ledge overlooking a steaming pit. "Where's your fancy star-magic now? Can't blast your way out of this one, can you? Can't conjure a mountain to fall on me here, eh?" He laughed, a harsh, grating sound that grated on Xylar's raw nerves. "You lost one family, you foolish alien. Now watch as I take this one too. Your little crew, waiting outside like pathetic pups, hoping their false god will save them. They'll be next, once I'm done with you."

The words cut deeper than any blade, slicing through Xylar's resolve. He stumbled, the weight of his inadequacy crushing him, the memory of Elara's dying face flashing before his eyes. He was struggling, desperately trying not to be overwhelmed. The relentless clang of steel, the suffocating heat, Malakor's venomous taunts – it all pressed down on him, a suffocating weight that threatened to extinguish his very will to fight. He remembered the faces of Elara and her crew, then the faces of Grog, Lyra, Finn, Rory, and Pip. He had promised them. He had promised himself. But the skill gap was too vast, the monster too powerful, too ingrained in this world of violence. Hope began to dwindle, flickering like a dying flame. Malakor's massive blade seemed to fill his vision, a dark, unstoppable force descending for the kill.

The pirate captain, seeing the despair in Xylar's eyes, raised his sword for the finishing blow, a triumphant snarl twisting his face, already tasting victory. Xylar braced himself, his energy flagging, his muscles screaming in protest, accepting the inevitable.

But before Redtooth's blade began its downward arc, a cacophony of familiar voices, distant yet impossibly clear, filled the very air of the caldera. They were faint at first, carried on the erratic drafts of the volcanic chamber, but Xylar's advanced auditory senses, capable of filtering immense noise and picking out specific frequencies, identified them instantly. To Malakor, the cacophony of steam, rock, and clashing steel would have drowned out anything, but to Xylar, his crew's voices were a sharp, undeniable beacon, cutting through the chaos. They quickly swelled, filling the space with an impossible warmth, a defiant roar that shook the very ground.

"Xylar! Use his weight! He's too slow to recover after a heavy swing!" That was Grog, his booming voice, a rumble of thunder, cutting through the despair, reminding Xylar of Malakor's inherent disadvantage.

"Don't give him an opening, Cap'n! Remember the feint! Draw him in!" Finn's precise, calm advice, a beacon of tactical brilliance amidst the chaos.

"He telegraphs! Watch his shoulder! Drive him to the steam vents! Blind him!" Lyra's sharp, strategic insights pinpoint Malakor's tells and a weakness in the environment.

"For The Space Serpent! For all of us! Fight, Captain!" Rory's rallying cry, infused with his own hard-won courage, echoed the collective will of his family.

The voices of his crew, his family, filled the caldera, an unbreakable chorus of loyalty and support. They weren't just sounds; they were anchors, lifelines thrown across the abyss of his despair, pulling him back from the brink. They weren't just shouting encouragement; they were giving him actionable advice, their combined wisdom flooding his alien mind, translating directly into battle strategies.

A surge of warmth, a fierce, protective love, ignited within Xylar, burning away the cold tendrils of fear. He was not alone. They had risked everything, disobeyed his direct order, just to be there for him, to offer him their strength, their belief. The despair vanished, replaced by a cold, burning resolve, a determination he hadn't known he possessed. The fatigue that had threatened to overwhelm him receded, replaced by a strange, alien vigor. He was no master swordsman, but he had the heart of a captain, and the unwavering support of a family that spanned worlds. He tightened his grip on his cutlass, his knuckles white. Malakor's downward strike was still coming, but Xylar saw it now, truly saw it. He would not just dodge. He would fight back. He slowly started to fight back, not with brute force, but with a cunning born of desperation, a newly ignited fire, and the unwavering voices of his crew guiding his every move, every parry, every counter-attack. The tide, imperceptibly at first, had begun to turn.

Chapter 44: The Tide Turns

Fueled by the echoing voices of his crew and a fierce, protective love for his new family, Xylar underwent a profound transformation. The initial fear that had threatened to consume him evaporated, replaced by a cold, calculating resolve. He was still not a master swordsman, but his alien mind, now unburdened by despair, processed Malakor's every move with astounding clarity. He saw the subtle shifts in Malakor's weight, the telegraphing twitches of his shoulder before a heavy blow, and the slight overextension that accompanied a confident thrust.

Malakor, roaring in fury at Xylar's continued resistance, unleashed another sweeping, bone-shattering strike. Xylar didn't just parry; he met the blade not with strength, but with a precise redirection, using Malakor's own momentum against him. The pirate, caught off balance, stumbled slightly, his heavy frame momentarily unwieldy on the jagged rock.

"He's got a blind spot on his left, Cap'n! Just after that big swing!" Lyra's sharp voice cut through the clamor. As Malakor recovered, Xylar seized the opportunity, pushing past his guard with a quick, unexpected jab. It wasn't a powerful strike, but it forced Malakor to twist awkwardly, exposing his flank.

"Use the heat, Xylar! Drive him into the steam!" Finn's calm, tactical voice echoed, his keen eye identifying a dangerous environmental hazard. Seeing Malakor's stumble and exposure, Xylar pressed his advantage. He lunged forward, not with a direct attack, but with a series of quick, harassing jabs, forcing Malakor to react, to move, to concede ground. He feinted left, then right, drawing the pirate away from the open ground and towards a cluster of narrow, hissing steam vents. Malakor, bellowing in frustration, followed, his massive sword whistling through the air.

The air around the vents shimmered with heat and sulfurous mist. Xylar, now moving with a newfound, fluid cunning, expertly sidestepped a powerful overhead chop. As Malakor's blade embedded itself momentarily in the unforgiving rock, Xylar didn't hesitate. He pulled Malakor forward with a sudden, unexpected tug on his blade, forcing the pirate directly into the scalding steam.

A guttural cry of pain erupted from Malakor as the superheated vapor enveloped him. He reeled back, momentarily blinded and disoriented, clutching his face. It was the first true injury Xylar had inflicted, a raw burn across Malakor's exposed skin, and it sent a surge of grim satisfaction through him.

"Stay on him, Cap'n! Don't let him breathe!" Rory's voice, raw with urgency, spurred him on. Xylar didn't let up. He became a whirlwind of motion, no longer merely defending, but actively attacking, exploiting Malakor's temporary vulnerability. He used the treacherous terrain to his advantage, leaping onto higher rocks, striking from unexpected angles, then retreating before Malakor could fully recover his bearings. He targeted Malakor's larger limbs—his sword arm, his legs— not seeking fatal blows, but aiming to cripple, to slow.

Chapter 45: The Final Battle

The battle raged on, a brutal exchange of steel and will. Malakor, roaring in pure fury as the steam dissipated, fought with renewed, desperate savagery, his attacks becoming even more wild and unpredictable. His blade, a terrifying arc of steel, smashed against the rocks, trying to break Xylar's guard, to crush him through sheer force. He managed to land a few glancing blows on Xylar – a painful scrape along his arm, a bruising thud against his ribs – but Xylar, now fueled by an unshakeable determination, barely registered the pain. His alien physiology, combined with the sheer force of his will, pushed him beyond human limits.

He focused on Malakor's over-reliance on brute strength. "He's putting all his weight behind that swing, Xylar! Counter his pivot!" Grog's words replayed in his mind. Xylar baited Malakor into powerful, open swings, then twisted out of the way, making the pirate expend valuable energy and expose himself. He aimed for the joint, the knee, the elbow—the vulnerable points his crew had shown him in their hasty training.

A sharp clang echoed as Xylar's blade, guided by Finn's precision, slid beneath Malakor's guard, scoring a shallow but painful cut across the pirate's sword arm. Malakor roared, more in frustration than pain, a thin line of blood welling from the wound. Redtooth was injured, but still fought, his eyes burning with renewed hatred, now mixed with a growing, disbelieving fury.

The tide had truly turned. Xylar, once overwhelmed, was now dancing around Malakor, a dark phantom in the swirling steam and dim light. He wasn't just surviving; he was winning. He pressed Malakor relentlessly, driving him back towards the very center of the caldera, where the jagged rocks provided more cover for Xylar's agile movements.

Finally, with a cunning feint that Malakor, in his rage, failed to recognize, Xylar created an opening. He lunged forward, not to strike, but to clash blades with a resounding impact. Then, with a practiced twist, a move Lyra had demonstrated countless times, Xylar used Malakor's own force against him, leveraging the pirate's weight to twist the blade from his grasp. With a final, desperate heave, the massive, wickedly curved sword spun through the air, landing with a dull clatter on the obsidian floor, far out of Malakor's reach. Before Malakor could fully register his loss, Xylar's own blade, precise and swift, found its mark. He sliced a deep, incapacitating gash across Malakor's exposed leg. The pirate captain staggered, a guttural cry of defeat escaping his lips as he finally collapsed onto the jagged rocks, utterly vanquished at Xylar's feet.

Chapter 46: How The Mighty Have Fallen

Xylar stood over the now disarmed pirate, his cutlass still clutched in his hand, its tip pointed at Malakor's throat. Redtooth Malakor, the once-feared pirate lord, the beast who had terrorized the seas, was finally injured and defeated, brought to his knees, panting, humiliated, his face streaked with sweat, grime, and blood, his eyes wide with a dawning, terrifying realization.

Xylar's voice, though quiet, resonated with a chilling power that filled the caldera, stripping Malakor of his last vestiges of control. "You thought this was a game, Malakor? You thought this was just about ships and plunder? You reduced lives to numbers, and suffering to sport." Xylar lowered his blade slightly, pressing the tip against Malakor's chest, where the tattered remnants of his shirt lay open. "I was an observer. A scientist. My purpose was knowledge, understanding. But you changed me. You murdered my first family – Elara, her crew, and the Sea Serpent. You ripped them from the world with a cruelty I, in my innocence, could barely comprehend. You took everything from me, leaving me adrift and lost."

His eyes, in the dim, fiery light, seemed to glow with an inner luminescence, revealing the alien power beneath the human facade, a cold, cosmic judgment. "You thought you'd extinguished my purpose, left me nothing but an empty shell.

But what you didn't know, Malakor, is that from broken things, new, stronger things can be born. From the wreckage of the Sea Serpent, a new ship rose – The Space Serpent, a testament to what happens when two worlds, two technologies, two different kinds of courage, combine. From my shattered mission, a new, righteous purpose was forged. And from the ashes of my past, a new family was born – the one you hear now, the one that screamed my name, that fed me their strength, that gave me the will to stand here, over you."

Xylar's voice deepened, cold and unwavering, growing in power until it filled the infernal chamber. "You terrorized, you plundered, you destroyed. You reveled in the screams of the innocent and the despair of the helpless. You thought you were untouchable, a god of the waves, above consequence. But every soul you crushed, every village you burned, every man, woman, and child you murdered – they all whispered your name into the ether. And those whispers carried across the very fabric of existence, across dimensions, across worlds, drawing judgment closer to your wicked heart. You believed you were above reckoning, above justice."

He pressed the blade infinitesimally closer. "But this is your reckoning, Malakor. This is your justice. This is what you had coming for all those you terrorized. For every tear shed, every dream shattered, every life violently extinguished. You are about to face the true consequence of your monstrous deeds. And you will find that a beast, no matter how grand, how terrifying, how seemingly invincible, can be slain. Not by another beast, but by a scientist, turned captain, turned avenger. By a man who learned to fight, driven by the memory of one family, and the unwavering love of another. Your reign of terror ends here, Malakor. And I will be the one to ensure it."

Chapter 47: The Beast Slain, A New Oath Forged

With a swift, firm motion, fueled by the countless lives Redtooth Malakor had so cruelly extinguished, Xylar brought his cutlass down. It was a single, precise stroke, delivered with all the weight of vengeance, all the sorrow of the lost, and all the love for the family he now held dear. The blade, sharp and true, severed Malakor's head clean. The sound that followed was stark, brutal, and absolute: the dull thud of the pirate lord's severed head hitting the obsidian floor, quickly followed by the heavy, lifeless fall of his once formidable body.

The vast caldera, moments before a crucible of fire and fury, became utterly still. The flickering flames cast long, dancing shadows over the grim tableau. The only sounds were the distant hiss of geothermal vents and the faint, unsettling crackle of dying embers. For a long, breathless moment, the very air seemed to hold its breath, processing the death of a monster.

Then, the silence was shattered.

From the fissure, from the depths of the mountain, a deafening eruption of cheers and praise tore through the air. The shouts of Xylar's crew, raw with triumph and relief, filled the chamber, echoing off the jagged walls. They had heard the final, decisive blow. They knew. The once-feared pirate lord, Redtooth Malakor, was finally, irrevocably slain. The terror he had sown across the seas had come to its brutal, definitive end.

Xylar stood over the fallen tyrant, his chest heaving, the cutlass still in his hand. He looked down at the lifeless form, a profound sense of closure, yet also a chilling emptiness, washing over him. The thirst for vengeance, so long a burning inferno within him, had finally been quenched.

He moved then, his eyes scanning the fallen pirate. As a token for the struggle and suffering Malakor had inflicted, Xylar took a few of his personal possessions: the wickedly crafted, blood-stained dagger from Malakor's belt, a heavy, intricate gold ring from his finger, and a worn, leather-bound logbook from his satchel, perhaps containing the secrets of his plunders, or merely the records of his depravity.

Having delivered his final judgment, Xylar turned to face the entrance to the caldera, where the triumphant cheers of his crew still echoed. His voice, weary but swelling with a new kind of power, a resonance born of hard-won victory and collective purpose, addressed them all within the cavern.

"He is done! Redtooth Malakor, the monster who plagued these waters, will terrorize no more! He thought he could break us, extinguish hope, and claim dominion through fear!" Xylar's gaze swept over their faces, illuminated by the dawning light filtering into the caldera. "But he underestimated the human spirit. He underestimated friendship. He underestimated family! He underestimated the Space Serpent!"

He raised his cutlass, then pointed it out towards the vast, open ocean visible through the fissure's mouth. "The reign of terror on the sea is over! For too long, fear has been Malakor's greatest weapon. But today, we bury that fear with him! We reclaim the waves! From this day forward, let the whisper on the winds be of courage, of justice, and of hope!"

His voice deepened, echoing with a new, profound purpose. "We came for vengeance, and we found it. But in doing so, we found something more. We learned that the world needs more than just vengeance. It needs protection. There are still shadows on these seas, still those who would prey on the innocent. Malakor was one monster, but the world is vast, and darkness can hide in many forms."

He looked at each of his crew members, his gaze steady and filled with a quiet challenge. "We are The Space Serpent. A ship born of two worlds, wielded by a family forged in fire and loyalty. We are fast. We are strong. And we are just. My original mission was to observe. But my new mission, our new mission, is to protect. To be a beacon of hope against the encroaching shadows. We will sail these seas not for plunder, but for principle. Not for terror, but for justice. We will be the guardians of the waves, the unexpected defenders against the darkness that still lurks beneath the surface."

"Will you sail with me, not just as a crew seeking revenge, but as a force for good?"

A final, resounding roar of agreement erupted from his crew, even louder than their cheers for Malakor's demise. "Aye, Cap'n!" Grog bellowed, his voice filled with pride. Lyra nodded, a fierce smile on her lips. Finn gripped his cutlass, his commitment silent but absolute.

Chapter 48: An Embrace and a New Adventure

With their new oath forged in the belly of the beast, Xylar emerged alone from the hot, unsettling caldera, stepping back into the cooler, crisp air of the island. He took a deep, steadying breath, the scent of salt and damp earth a welcome contrast to the sulfur and blood of the cavern. The weight of Malakor's final judgment still lingered, a solemn echo in his mind, but it was quickly being replaced by a profound sense of lightness, of purpose.

The moment he truly exited the fissure, he was immediately enveloped in the eager embrace of his loving and faithful crew. Grog, his face split by a triumphant grin, clapped Xylar on the back with a force that nearly buckled his knees. "You did it, Cap'n! You actually did it!" Lyra, her eyes shining with unshed tears of relief, pulled him into a fierce, relieved hug, her grip tight as if to confirm he was truly there, truly safe. Finn offered a rare, genuine smile and a firm handshake, a silent acknowledgment of their shared triumph and the heavy burden Xylar had carried. Rory, his eyes no longer haunted by past injustices, simply nodded, a deep satisfaction settling over his features, the grim shadow of Malakor finally lifted from his soul. Pip, bouncing on the balls of his feet, cheered loudest of all, his youthful energy unbounded, radiating pure joy.

The warmth of their embrace, the strength of their loyalty, was a far greater prize than any treasure Malakor possessed. The vengeance was complete, the beast slain, and with his demise, the suffocating pall of terror that had gripped the seas for so long began to lift. Xylar could almost feel the air lighten, the distant ocean murmuring with a new, hopeful whisper rather than the old shriek of fear. Their journey for retribution had ended, but the family remained, stronger than ever, ready to face whatever new horizons awaited the Space Serpent, now transformed from a vessel of personal vengeance into a legend in the making. Their true adventure had just begun.

A Night of Celebration

As the immediate jubilation subsided, Xylar led his triumphant landing party back through the island's winding paths. The trek was filled with chatter and laughter, a stark contrast to the grim determination of their earlier ascent. Reaching the shore, the sight of the Space Serpent riding the gentle waves, bathed in the soft glow of the setting sun, was a welcome beacon. Jett, Reef, and the rest of the crew waiting on deck burst into renewed cheers as their captain and his victorious team clambered aboard.

That night, the deck of The Space Serpent transformed into a vibrant scene of celebration. A feast was laid out, tables laden with fresh seafood, preserved meats, and whatever exotic fruits they had managed to procure from their last port. Tankards clinked, songs were sung, and the air hummed with an almost palpable sense of relief and camaraderie. Even Xylar, usually reserved, found himself laughing freely, sharing tales of the battle with his eager crew. He watched them, his new family, their faces illuminated by the flickering lanterns and the rising moon. This was the life he had built from the ashes, a testament to resilience and the enduring power of connection.

The Logbook's Secret

Long after the last song faded and the crew had retired, their celebratory exhaustion pulling them into deep slumber, Xylar remained awake. He sat alone in his cabin, the gentle creak of the ship his only companion, and finally pulled out Malakor's worn, leather-bound logbook. Its contents had been a nagging curiosity, a loose end in the knot of vengeance, and now, with peace settled over him, it was time to unravel it.

The pages were old, some brittle, filled with Malakor's crude, almost illegible scrawl. Many were indeed simple, depraved records of plunder and destruction. But as Xylar delved deeper, his analytical mind, honed by years of scientific observation, began to discern a pattern. Interspersed with the ravings were intricate diagrams and strange, swirling symbols. He found detailed, hand-drawn maps, unlike any he had ever seen, charting currents and coastlines that didn't correspond to known geographies. Alongside these were pages filled with cryptic notes about specific artifacts or 'keys' — a unique type of compass, a crystal that hummed with a strange energy, a shard of an ancient star-chart.

As he pieced together the fragments, a thrilling, terrifying possibility began to emerge. These weren't just pirate maps; they seemed to be instructions, guiding steps toward a mythical 'Crimson Isle', a place rumored only in the darkest legends of the sea. Malakor hadn't just been a pirate; he had been obsessed with finding something far grander, far more dangerous. The logbook described the island as a place of immense power, guarding an untold treasure, but also cursed by a perilous force.

Xylar leaned back in his chair, the flickering lantern light glinting off the pages. The vengeance he sought was fulfilled, but Malakor, even in death, had offered him a new challenge, a new purpose. This wasn't about plunder for him, but about discovery, about understanding the unknown. The implications of these maps and keys were immense, hinting at a world far more complex and mysterious than even his alien origins had prepared him for. He closed the logbook, the weight of its secrets heavy in his hands.

The Space Serpent had buried the fear of Malakor. Now, it seemed, she was destined to sail toward a new dawn, chasing a legend, guarding the balance between wonder and peril. What secrets did the Crimson Isle truly hold? And what new trials awaited Captain Xylar and his extraordinary crew on their next grand adventure? Only the uncharted waters and the cryptic clues of Malakor's logbook would tell.

About the Author

For Teak Drewett-Tyson, the call of fantasy and adventure has always been powerful. Growing up under the vast, star-dusted skies of the Arizona desert, he was captivated by the endless expanse, fostering a deep wonder for what lies beyond the known. This fascination, combined with a lifelong love for epic tales, fueled the worlds he built in his mind and now shares in this book. A devoted husband and father, Teak thanks you for joining him on this adventure.